Purrr

Skye MacKinnon

CONTENTS

Five signs a cat is in heat:

- Rubs against anything male
- Coos over kittens
- Presents her assets as often as possible
- Gets easily distracted
- Loses interest in assassinations

Kill me now. This is going to be hell.

The third book in this purrfectly exciting urban fantasy series.

A QUICK WORD BEFORE WE GET STARTED

As you will know from the previous two books, this series is set in a world very similar to our own, but there are some deciding differences. Technology has developed differently, and while there are many devices you may be used to, such as televisions, there are no mobile phones, cars or the internet. No guns, either.

This book is written in British English and uses some British expressions and idioms. Please don't see these as spelling mistakes. We say mum rather than mom, use a lot of 's' instead of 'z' (cosy, realise, …) and use 'got' as the past participle of 'get' (instead of 'gotten').

And finally, subscribe to Skye's newsletter for updates about new releases: skyemackinnon.com/newsletter.

You'll even get a free book for subscribing, so it's totally worth it.

Dedicated to the Terrace Coffee House, without which many of my books would never get written. Thanks for all the cream on my hot chocolate.

M.E.O.W.
WE KILL SO YOU DON'T HAVE TO.

CHAPTER ONE

"You really need to shave."

I blink up at Lily, still too tired to make much sense of what she's just said. Since when does Lily give me personal hygiene advice?

"Seriously, look in the mirror and then take a razor. Not mine, though."

She dances away, swaying her hips like the succubus she is. Ever since she returned from that convention, she's been spreading seduction and allure. It's a miracle that nobody in this house has ended up in bed with her yet. I hope.

I groan and slide out of my hammock. I've been sleeping a lot in the past three days, but it never seems to be enough. My body is changing, turning against me, and I don't know how to stop it. Right now, Ryker is the only one who can even understand what I'm saying. I still meow every time I open my mouth, which means I rarely speak nowadays. It's too frustrating to see them trying not to laugh at my frantic meows. And then there's the purring. My body does it whenever I feel the tiniest flicker of happiness. It's the reason why I've stayed away from the men. They don't need to know that I'm happy when I'm around them. The exception is Ryker because I need him to translate for me.

I've never been a chatterbox but knowing that I need someone else to pass on my messages has made me think twice about what I want to say. What actually needs to be said. And surprisingly, that's not a lot at all. My employees know what to do, they don't need much help or encouragement. They're running the place while I'm…indisposed. So far, none of them has come to me with any problems, which means either there aren't any or that they don't want to bother me. Or they're scared of me. Who knows.

I take Lily's advice and stagger over to the dusty mirror hanging from a nail on one of the wooden posts supporting my hammock. I never really use it. Vanity is for losers. The only thing I care about is looking threatening when I need to. I don't need to be pretty.

Still, I can't help but gasp when I see myself. This must be a nightmare. My face is covered in black hair, as midnight black as my panther fur. Except that I should be human. I shouldn't have fur on my face. And my eyes shouldn't be ringed with yellow either.

Am I turning into some kind of hybrid? Part cat, part human? It's what I've always been inside, especially since my collar was lifted, but it's not what I should look like. I need to blend in. I can't do my job looking like a mutant.

A razor. Lily said I should shave. Where did I put

that razor… I've not used it in ages. My body has very little hair growth, and I don't really care about the few tiny hairs on my legs. It's not as if anyone gets to see them when I'm wearing my black leather trousers. But now, I really need to do something about my hair growth.

I run a hand over my cheeks. They're actually furry. No, a razor won't do much good here. Even my forehead is covered in black hair, about as long as my pinkie nail. I look like a cat on two legs. I shudder. This can't be happening.

Even my teeth feel different. I run my tongue over my front incisors. Sharp. Pointy. Panther.

I groan and go back to my hammock. I'm not going to leave the attic today. Maybe by tomorrow, everything will be back to normal. An assassin can hope.

I smell Ryker's scent before he sticks his head up the attic trapdoor. I've left it open, lacking the energy to get up and close it. I turn away from him and pull my blanket over my head. I don't want him to see me like this. Maybe I should shift, but who knows what might happen then? I might end up as a furless panther with human skin. That would be even worse than being a hairy human.

"Lily told me you might want some company," he says cheerily.

That bitch. Does she seriously think I'd want anyone to see me in this state? Lily needs a reality check. Not everyone is an exhibitionist like her.

"Go away," I meow. At least I can talk to Ryker. He understands my meows, even when he's human.

"I don't think so. I'm bored."

Great. A bored cat. There's nothing worse. Usually, that ends in destroyed curtains and torn open catnip bags.

He plops down on the bright orange beanbag in the corner. My latest acquisition; it was only delivered two days ago, but I've not really been in the mood to enjoy it. In fact, I've only sat on it once, then decided moping felt better in my hammock.

"This is comfy. Now, tell me, what's wrong?"

I snort. "Besides being stuck in this state? Besides knowing what I know?"

He chuckles, ignoring the sarcasm in my voice. "Yes, besides that. We'll find a solution, don't worry. You'll be back to normal in no time."

"I'll never be normal again. All my life has been a lie. I'm not even real."

I hear him get up and approach. He's so close that all I can smell is his intoxicating scent. I try not to breathe it in. It's intense and makes me want to do things that wouldn't be appropriate. Ever since he's turned human for the first time, his scent has changed. Before, when he was a cat, he wasn't of interest to my ovaries, but now, when he's close like this, I have to suppress what I don't want to feel.

He puts a hand on my shoulder, and I try not to flinch. I don't want him to touch me. I'm a clone, an abomination, and right now I'm covered in fur. I just want to be alone and wallow in justified self-pity.

"What's wrong?" he repeats. "Talk to me, Kat. You don't need to go through this alone."

I stay quiet. There's nothing to say. He's wrong. I have to go through this on my own. Once I'm back to normal, I'm going back to the Pack headquarters to find out the truth about my heritage, to see if there are more of us, more clones, and then I'm going to shut them down once and for all.

"How's little Kat?" I ask instead of an answer.

"Fine, last I heard. She's been asking to see you though."

My clone – no, not my clone, she's not modelled after me after all – has been staying with Gryphon's aunt while I'm recovering. I've never met that aunt, but if Gryphon thinks she's trustworthy, then I'm alright with that. None of us has experience with looking after a child. Benjamin is almost a child still himself, Bethany is terribly immature, and Lily is busy running Meow as my second-in-command. Ryker, Lennox and Gryphon have been here at our headquarters almost the entire time, but they're not fit to parent a child either, no matter how grown up she might act. Little Kat has never had a childhood, she's never been allowed to play, and Gryphon said that his aunt might help the girl adjust to normal life. Rose, that's her name. Aunt Rose. She has two grown-up daughters herself so she knows what she's doing.

"Shall I tell her she can come to visit?"

"No," I snap immediately, sounding harsher than I intended. Ryker hasn't seen my face yet. He'll understand when he sees me. If I let him.

"Okay, don't get all worked up. Let's keep a visit for once you're feeling better. How's the chest?"

I rub my sternum where Gryphon managed to crack two of my ribs while resuscitating me. My body isn't healing as quickly as it should. I'm broken and I don't know how to fix myself.

"Getting better," I lie. It still hurts like hell when I touch it. "I hope Gryphon isn't feeling guilty still?"

Ryker chuckles. "I don't think he's going to stop feeling guilty until you're walking around healthy and happy. Lennox is still blaming himself as well. This whole house is filled with nothing but self-pity and self-loathing."

He sounds bitter about it, and I realise that I've never properly talked to him about his new human self. I've simply accepted that he can now shift, that he's found his human side.

"How are you?" I ask softly.

In response, he gently squeezes my shoulder. "It's confusing. I thought it would be hard to walk on two legs, to talk with humans, but it's like I've been doing it all my life. I still don't like looking at mirrors though. That face doesn't belong to me. In my mind, I'm still a cat."

"We have that in common," I mutter. "I don't want to see myself in the mirror, either."

"Show me." His voice is a quiet demand, hitting my senses at the same time as another burst of his scent.

I find myself turning before I can stop myself. I swipe my hair out of my face and let him look at me.

I was expecting surprise. Disgust. Horror at my

ugliness. Instead, he slowly reaches out and strokes my cheek.

"You're beautiful," he whispers. "Exquisite."

Of all the reactions I imagined, this wasn't one of them. I don't know how to respond. I stare at him in confusion.

He chuckles. "Did you think I'd run away screaming?"

I nod, unable to speak at seeing the heat in his gaze.

"It makes your eyes seem brighter," he whispers and kneels on the floor so that we're on the same level. His mouth is close to mine, too close, but I'm stuck in my hammock and can't move away.

"You're beautiful," he repeats. "You shouldn't try and hide the cat in you. You're both, cat and human, and you need to give her space to unfold, especially now."

"Especially now?" I repeat, confused.

He quirks an eyebrow. "You don't know? I can smell it from half a mile away."

"What?"

"Does that mean this doesn't happen every time? Is it the first time you have this fur on your face?"

"I have no clue what you're on about," I say, repressing a frustrated growl. If he's not going to tell me what's going on this very second, I'm going to bite his head off with my overly sharp human teeth. Or maybe some other bits that are easier to bite off than a head.

"Estrus," he replies gently. "Surely this isn't your first time?"

That word sounds familiar, but I don't want to believe what I think it means.

"You're in heat," he explains, confirming my fears. "I thought you knew." He clears his throat. "How can you not know? Every cat in the area will know by now. Your scent is rather strong."

I glare at him. "Are you telling me that I smell?"

He winces. "No, not smell. Your scent is that of the most fragrant rose, delicate and strong at the same time, full of promises of beauty and happiness." He gives me a small smile, tinged with a trace of embarrassment. "I've had my cats spread the message that you're not a normal female, that you're out of bounds, but there are dozens of males leaving their marks down below in the courtyard."

I squeeze my eyes shut, wanting to escape. And I here I was thinking it couldn't get any worse. How wrong I was.

I'm in heat. That would explain the fur, the meowing, how I don't feel right in my own skin. Maybe it even explains the dream I had while being unconscious, the one where I fucked Gryphon on the floor. I'd blush at the thought if my cheeks weren't covered in black fur.

"How?" I stammer. "Why?"

"I'm not exactly an expert," Ryker hedges, "but I assume the collar triggered it, or maybe nearly dying. Maybe your body has realised that it's time to pass on your genes."

I open my eyes just in time to see an amused smile spread on his face. "I'm not going to have kittens," I protest. "My body can stop being in heat and go back to normal. I'm not interested in having offspring."

His smile only grows at my words. "I believe humans have ways to prevent having kittens. You don't need to get pregnant to get better."

I stare at him. "Are you saying I need sex to feel better?" I point at my hairy face. "To make this go away?"

"I think so. It's not exactly like I've got any experience with shifter females in heat, but that's what normal cats do. If you prolong it, if you don't give in to your urges, you'll go crazy, and rub against furniture, spray every street corner, howl all night, that sort of thing. Better to deal with it before it gets worse."

"That feels wrong," I mutter. "Having sex just to get better. I'd feel like I'm exploiting whoever I sleep with."

His smile wavers a little. "It wouldn't have to be the only reason. I know of at least three men who'd be happy to assist you."

I'm sure he can see my blush through my fur now. Three men. How did he come to this conclusion?

Lennox, he probably knows about him. Gryphon… did I say anything when I woke up? Did I moan while being unconscious, while dreaming that I was with him?

And who's the third?

Is it…?

His lips meet mine.

CHAPTER TWO

For someone who's never kissed before, or at least hasn't kissed a human, he's overwhelmingly good. His lips are soft and supple, yet his kiss is hard and passionate. He cups my face, drawing me closer as he claims my mouth. I barely register that he's touching my furry face; the kiss is too intense to focus on anything else. Our tongues dance in a fight for survival, our breaths meet each other in ragged, short blows.

My entire body is tingling, aching to be touched. I claw at his back, pulling him closer, but then the hammock turns and suddenly we're on the floor, me on top of him, his hands still on my face, his lips somehow still on mine.

Laughter breaks from his throat and I smile against his kiss, but I don't stop. Can't stop. My skin is on fire, needs to be touched, needs to be soothed. I moan when his hands slip beneath my shirt. Yes, that's it. More of that. I need more, so much more.

"Fuck me," I whisper breathlessly, before devouring his mouth once again. I'm taking control now, I'm the one setting the pace. I straddle him, pushing him flat down onto the floor, rocking against his hips, his hardness. My fingernails turn into claws, sharp and brutal, and I slash away his shirt, leaving red scratches on his dark skin. He can take it. He's a cat, he knows that we can be wild when it comes to sex.

His chest is broad, his abs like a marble statue. I run my fingers over his smooth skin, revelling in the sensation. His yellow eyes look up at me, mesmerised.

"Mine," I growl, then rip my own shirt from my body, bra and all, until I'm naked for him. My skin is covered in black fur, shimmering in the dim light, but I don't care. It only turns me on even more, to see what a predator I am. I'm a hunter and he is my prey.

I bend forward and kiss him once more. Our lips clash, teeth against teeth, tongues against tongues. This isn't a romantic dance, this is a fight, a war for dominance.

Suddenly, I'm on my back and he's on top of me, his massive body pinning me down. He grabs my wrists and pushes them above my head, exposing my body to him. I glare into his amber eyes, the colour of honey and sunshine. I could fight him and I'd probably win, but I want to see what he does. He flashes me a grin, then takes my nipple into his mouth, sucking, nibbling, biting. I moan at the sweet pain, craving more. He takes my sounds as encouragement and bites my breast, his teeth sinking deep into my skin. I buckle beneath him, groaning as bliss races through my body, all the way into my toes, reaching every inch of me.

I need him inside me. This isn't enough.

He bites my other breast, leaving his marks on my skin. I feel blood trickle down my skin and it turns me on to new heights. The pain mixes with my pleasure, creating new things in my twisted mind.

"My turn," I growl and flip him over. He gasps in surprise, not expecting my strength to match his. I turn, crouching above him, my thighs pressed against his ribs, my head above the prize. A little more careful this time, I slice through his jeans, my claws sharp enough to cut the fabric without a problem.

I smile, the predator in me coming to the surface. There he is. Hard and ready for me. Still smiling, I lower myself, my arms on his thighs, until he's in reach. I kiss his tip, licking away the first drops of desire. He groans and tries to move, but I press my thighs against his chest, making sure he stays the way he is.

I take him into my mouth, but I'm not gentle. My teeth scrape his skin, eliciting sounds that spurn me on to take him deeper, almost swallowing him. His hips jerk up, making me gag, but I love it, love every moment.

The tingling in my body has turned into flames, burning through my veins, erasing any restraint that I may have shown. I straighten, rip a hole into my sweat pants with a swipe of my claws, tear at my panties and lower myself onto him. He groans in surprise, but I push down, taking him without giving myself the time to adjust. He's big, almost too much so, but the pain is what I need, what I crave.

I sway my hips, slowly at first, then fast, fucking him, taking him, claiming him.

Our groans and pants merge into a beautiful song, lifting my spirits, carrying me to the heights of pleasure before letting me tumble down the waterfall, in his arms, together.

❄ ❄ ❄ ❄ ❄ ❄

*C*OLD EYES STARE DOWN AT ME. *I* DON'T RECOGNISE THE *man. The lower half of his face is hidden behind a mask, but his eyes are enough to make me shake with fright. Evil glints in his black pupils, cold ice in the blue around them. I try to move, but there is metal around my wrists and ankles, holding me in place. I fight against my bonds, but I dimly remember that I've been here before, that I never manage to escape. I'm trapped.*

"Don't worry, it will be over soon," the man whispers, but it's not reassuring me. On the contrary, the fear paralysing me is only getting worse.

"And you won't even remember this ever happened." His eyes narrow as she smiles underneath the mask.

No, I have to remember. Traces of memories are flittering through my mind, of having been here before, hearing him say the same words, over and over. I can't forget this time. I mustn't. If I don't remember, I'm vulnerable. Ignorance could mean death.

He reaches up and lowers something metal down from the ceiling, some kind of machine. A light shines bright, too bright, and I close my eyes, even though I feel like I need to see what happens. If I don't see, I can't remember.

"This may hurt a little," the man says with a chuckle, and

then cold metal touches my forehead and the world explodes into screams.

A SCREAM MAKES ME SIT UP STRAIGHT. I LOOK FOR THE danger, the victim, but the only person in the room with me is Ryker, his body curled around me.

"Shhhh," he whispers and pulls me back down into his arms. "You were having a nightmare."

"But someone…"

Oh. It must have been me who screamed. Embarrassment clouds my mind. I never scream. I never let anyone know about my nightmares.

"Want to talk about it?"

His voice is soft and gentle, just like his eyes as he looks at me with sympathy.

I shake my head. "I don't even remember."

He nods and smiles. "Your fur has gone."

I touch my cheeks, surprised despite his words. Smooth skin greets me, no trace left of the fur that covered me before I fell asleep. In a way, I'm glad, but at the same time, I remember how Ryker looked at me with desire, how he craved me despite, or maybe because of, my feline side, and I almost wish the fur was back. The hunger inside of me is barely sated, despite spending hours with him inside me. A pleasant ache between my legs reminds me of what we did, how we joined.

Strangely enough, I'm okay with being in his arms. I

snuggle against him, barely recognising myself. I don't snuggle. I don't hug. I certainly don't fall asleep in a man's embrace. What the fuck is wrong with me? It must be the heat thing. It's making me soft, needy. I hope it passes soon.

"How long are cats in heat for?" I whisper, a little angry when he starts to grin.

"It can be weeks, months, who knows. Spaying helps, but I doubt you want that."

I resist the urge to protectively place my hands on my abdomen. "Nobody is touching my ovaries," I snarl.

He chuckles. "Didn't think so. Are there any other female shifters you could ask? Dogs go into heat too, right?"

I usually stay away from other shifters, mainly because they're all controlled by the Pack. The few who've managed to remain outside the Pack are either crazy or not powerful enough to be of any use.

"No," I admit, "but maybe Lennox knows someone."

I could ask him without mentioning the heat thing. I don't want everyone else to know, but I could innocently ask him if he has any female shifter friends. If he takes that as me being jealous, so be it.

"The only shifters I'm aware of are male," Ryker says with a regretful smile. "And as cats, we never much cared about what side they're on. They ignored us and we ignored them. Of course, that's going to change from now on."

I suddenly remember something I've wanted to ask for a while. "Pumpkin, is he a shifter too?"

His smile wavers. "I don't know and I have no idea how to find out. He's not shown any signs, but then, neither did I. I would never have known if you hadn't done that blood test. Maybe you could test him too?"

"Tell him to go to Bethany or Lily, they're the experts. I can draw blood, but I have no idea how to do the DNA comparison stuff."

He nods, hope flashing in his eyes. "Do you think it's likely? That he's a shifter even though he's got a cat mother?"

"Your guess is as good as mine." A yawn interrupts my words. "I need some tea or I'll fall asleep again."

He flashes me a grin. "I know something else that might keep you awake." His hand finds my breast and he squeezes gently. So different from last night. The scratches and bite marks he left have disappeared together with my fur.

Along with it, all the pains and aches left from almost dying – well, I actually died, my heart stopped according to Lily – have gone, making me feel better than I have in days. I might almost be ready to go downstairs and see what's been going on at Meow. Then I think of the stacks of paperwork likely waiting for me and decide to do more important things first. Like grabbing some food and tea.

I get up, leaving behind a disappointed Ryker. I smile at him. "Later. I'm starving."

Understanding seeps into his yellow eyes. "Do you want me to-"

I pull on some yoga pants and relief reflects on his

face. "You're getting up. You're going downstairs. That's good."

I chuckle. "Yes, that's good. I've got an assassin business to run, and more importantly, I've got the Pack to destroy once and for all."

CHAPTER THREE

I drink half the bottle of milk before even thinking about tea. Seems I'm still in cat mode. By the time the kettle is boiling, I'm sitting on the floor, the secret bag of catnip on my lap. Bliss. Almost as good as sex.

I no longer care about the tea, nor about the loud whistling of the kettle.

"Can someone please turn that off?"

Lily bursts into the kitchen, then breaks into laughter when she sees me on the floor.

"Are you high?"

I grin at her. "Not at all."

My mouth finds it hard to form the words, but that doesn't matter. I'm a happy cat. Yummy catnip.

"You can talk." Lily looks at me in surprise, and it takes me a moment to figure out why that shocks her.

"Oh. Yes. You can understand me."

Her eyes widen as she focuses on my mouth. "You're no longer meowing."

"Yes, I'm talking human again. Now leave me alone, stop guilt-tripping me."

Usually, this would be a big deal - I've got my voice back! - but the catnip is making it all seem unimportant. I'm going to need some more of it.

Lily sighs and takes the kettle off the flame and switches off the hob. "I think you need some coffee," she tells me sternly. "And my special detox smoothie."

I groan at the thought. I don't know what she puts into that concoction, but it smells and tastes disgusting. Plus, it takes away the woolly feeling the catnip gives me. I don't want it to go. I like this moment. I don't want it to end.

I pop another catnip cookie into my mouth. I make these whenever Lily is out of the house. She'd never let me bake them when she's around.

"Katriona Feln, I'm not letting you turn into an addict," she tells me and snatches the bag from my arms. The catnip makes me sluggish and my reflexes poor; that's the only reason why she manages to steal my treats. Maybe I've had a little too much after all. I can't let her take away my catnip.

I growl at her and flash some fang.

She chuckles. "You're adorable."

"Not the effect I was going for," I grumble, my words slurred. "Gimme back my catnip."

"No way. I need you coherent. There are things we need to discuss."

I stare at her blankly. What is there besides the joys of catnip that we need to talk about? It can't be important.

"Where is Ryker? I thought he was with you?" she asks with a wide grin. She must know that he's spent the night with me.

"With his cats. There was something he wanted to do… I can't remember."

Lily sighs. "I'm going to make that smoothie."

She basically has to force the smoothie down my throat, but once I've given my stomach time to settle, I'm kind of grateful for it. The clouds mulling my brain are slowly disappearing, giving way to clarity mixed with traces of embarrassment. I've let myself go, lost control. It seems I'm changing not just on the outside. If this continues, who knows what kind of person I'll end up as. A catnip addict, slothing on the sofa all day, unable to gather the energy to even do a single hit. No, not going to let that happen.

"Better?" Lily asks with a wry smile.

"Lots. Now, tell me, what's been happening with Meow?"

I'm glad she doesn't jab at me for not bothering with my business the past few days. She knows I would have been there if I could have.

"Nothing much. We've got a few new cases that might interest you, but nothing urgent, so I've left them on your desk. Benjamin thinks he's found a group of bank robbers that he's trying to join, so please get that idea out of his head. We need him to do our own robberies, not do it for other people. Bethany is locked in the lab, she's working on something and won't tell me what it is. Besides that, it's been quiet. Your men have been here almost every second of the day, though."

I almost spit out the last mouthful of smoothie. "My men?" I splutter. "You mean *the* men?"

She snickers. "Trust me, they're not interested in anyone but you. It's taken the combined effort of all of us to keep them from beleaguering you, watching over you at all times. I only let Ryker up there because of your hair problem." She winks at me. "Glad that one's sorted. You look a lot less weird now."

"Thanks. I better get some good razors if this happens again."

Lily laughs. "Let's hope it was a one-off. I love you, but I prefer you as a human. Without a catnip addiction."

She shoots me a stern glance, then walks off, leaving me to my own devices.

I put the empty smoothie jug in the sink, hoping that it will magically clean itself. I know, no such thing as house elves, but a cat can dream.

Lily said the men have been here most of the time, but now, the house is empty except for Lily and Bethany. I can hear Beth downstairs in the lab. A mysterious project? Call me intrigued.

The lab door is locked, making all sorts of alarm bells ring in my head. Nobody ever locks that door.

"Bethany?" I shout, putting on my stern boss voice. "Open up."

The sounds of her working stop, but the door doesn't open.

"Kat?" she asks, muffled through the thick metal door.

"You know it's me. Now let me in before I get angry."

She sighs and a moment later, the door opens, revealing a tired-looking Bethany. She's wearing a protective suit, turning my alarm bells into shrill sirens.

"What are you doing?"

I scan the lab behind her. The two workbenches are overflowing with equipment, so chaotic that I wonder what's Bethany turning into. Usually, she's so careful to keep everything tidy in here. The Bunsen burner behind her is still on, so I walk around her to switch it off. She moves to intercept me, but I'm faster, stepping to one side to see what she's been hiding behind her back.

"What is that?" I ask sharply, staring at the manila folder bearing the Pack logo embossed on the front. "What are you doing with Pack documents?"

She visibly cringes. "It's one of the files you guys brought back here. It's got some medical data that I've been wanting to explore..."

She doesn't meet my eyes.

"Medical data? Like what?"

"Cloning," she whispers. "Not to replicate any of it, of course," she adds quickly when I'm just about ready to shout at her. "Just to understand what they did and how. It might help me figure out what they did to you and to Little Kat. We might be able to know how many others were involved. How many other clones there are."

I'm tempted to reach out for the folder, but it's still

too fresh, too sore. I need more time to accept what I am. What they've done to me.

"I get that," I say slowly, "but what are you doing with all that equipment? Why aren't you just reading it? We would have done that eventually anyway."

"There are some bits that talk about a particular drug that was given to all clones, but it doesn't say what it actually did. I thought if I followed the instructions and made it, then maybe I'd understand..."

Her shoulders droop, but I don't let myself be deceived by that. "Were you planning to give this drug to me?" I ask sharply. "Or to Little Kat?"

Her eyes widen, reassuring me that her intentions weren't threatening. Thank the great cat in the sky.

"No, but once we have the drug, I thought I'd test your blood to see if there's any residue, even just the tiniest of traces. They gave it to you to have a lasting effect, permanent even, so I might be able to find evidence of that." Her expression hardens. "And if we ever find a clone who's not on our side... well, then we can test it on them."

I'm surprised by the steel in her voice. She's not a vengeful person. She likes to mess around, have fun with her poisons, but she's not enjoying other people's pain.

"Do you think we'll find other clones?"

She shrugs. "According to this, there are several dozen, but we seem to be missing any files that would tell us whether they're alive or not. They've been focusing a lot on Little Kat though, so I doubt many of the clones in between you and her are still around. Probably failed to meet their expectations."

I shudder. I still have no idea what their plans for me were, but seeing them experiment with kitten DNA to add that to shifters... not good. Mother nature is confused enough sometimes, we don't need humans meddling with that. Right now, I'm half human, half cat. If they added more cat, would that make me lose my humanity? Or worse, have they already done such a thing? Am I maybe not as human as I thought?

I push those thoughts away. They don't help, and I need a clear head to come up with what to do next.

"From now on, I want you to tell me exactly what you're doing with these files," I tell Beth sternly. She nods downtrodden, her eyes on the floor. "I know your intentions are good but we cannot let this information fall in the wrong hands. Or worse, let it corrupt us. We're going to stop them, not replicate their research, so once they're shut down, I want all of this destroyed."

She looks as if she wants to protest, but then nods. Somehow, I've got a feeling like we're going to have to talk about this again.

"Where are the other files that we got from the Pack lab?"

She points to a metal lockbox in one corner of the room. "Most of them are in there, but Gryphon's got some and I think Lennox too."

I groan. Great. The information is already spread all over the place. I trust Lennox, and yes, I think I trust Gryphon too, but I need to keep reminding myself that this is dangerous stuff. We can't risk any of those files getting lost, or worse, stolen.

"Until I know what information we have, none of

these are going to leave the house. I'm going to put that box into my office and if someone wants one of the folders, they'll have to come to me. Understood?"

"Can I keep this one?"

I sigh. "Yes, for now. But as I said, keep me informed of what you find out. And don't you dare ask me to be your guinea pig. Guinea cat."

She laughs softly. "I wouldn't dare to. I know you have claws."

If only she knew... those claws looked beautiful on Ryker's skin. Heat runs through my body, reminding me of the heat situation.

"Ehm, Bethany?"

"Yes?" Finally, she looks at me, her eyes filled with curiosity.

"I don't suppose you found anything on cat shifter reproductive physiology in there?"

Her eyebrows curve in amusement. "Are you having a painful period?"

I shouldn't have said anything.

"Not my period but... urgh, did you find anything?"

She shakes her head, a smile curving her lips. "No, but I'll let you know when I find something."

I nod stiffly and turn to leave. "Thanks."

Before I'm out of the door, she clears her throat. "I've got some extra strong pain killers and a hot water bottle, if you want."

I don't turn back. "No, thanks. Not that kind of problem."

If only she knew...

❧ ❧ ❧ ❧ ❧ ❧

My office is just like I left it, except that my in-tray has grown and had babies since I last stepped foot in this room. A few cases, Lily said. They're either all very long and detailed, or she's unable to count. Fun. At least this is a familiar task, something to get lost in, something to keep my mind off other things.

I sit down in my comfy leather chair and pull the first file from the pile. A woman wanting to get rid of her husband. I smile. And she wants him to suffer. Nice one. I put her on the priority stack.

The next three are business people wanting to have their competition eliminated. Low priority. They usually pay well but those cases are boring. There's no passion behind their motives, just cold calculations and maybe a touch of jealousy. Relationship murders are far more fun.

A man wanting his father killed. That's not unusual, but this time, it doesn't seem to be about an inheritance. The father is homeless, so I doubt he's got much money for the son to get. Why then would you want your own father murdered? There's no information on that in the document, so I put it on the priority stack, hoping that I'll get the time to deal with that case. It's unusual, which makes it mine.

After an hour, I've got three neat piles in front of me. High priority, low priority, and one breaking-and-entering pile for Benjamin. We're getting more and more of those requests every month. Ben is making a name for himself, or better, for Meow. It's a nice side business that gets us some extra money while also keeping the boy happy. He's not one for killing, but he excels at getting into places he shouldn't be in.

I feel a lot better now that I know what I can focus on in the coming days. A few fun, simple jobs, none of them connected to the Pack or other crime organisations. Just how it should be. Killing people for money. Wonderful.

I can deal with that.

What I can't deal with are the two men who've just entered the house.

CHAPTER FOUR

Gryphon and Lennox wait for me in the living room, as if they know that I'm no longer holed up in the attic. Well, both of them have exceptional senses, so I'm pretty sure they're aware of where in the house I am.

I feel like getting some tea, but then I'd have to make tea for all three of us and it would make them stay longer. I don't want to be around them for too long. Just the thought of those men makes heat pool between my legs. I hate it. Hate it so much. I'm clinging onto self-control as hard as I can, but my body is rebelling, fighting me at every step. If I let go, I'd dry-hump them on the sofa, then rip off their clothes and take them both at once. But that's not something Kat does. That's not me.

"You look a lot better," Gryphon observes when I enter the room. Lennox is spread out on one of the sofas, acting as if he lives here, but Gryphon is on the edge of his seat, as if he's not quite allowing himself to be comfortable.

I sit down opposite them, putting as much distance between us as I can. Even so, their scents fill my nose, causing tingles to race over my skin. My mouth waters at the thought of them being so close. I could get up and kiss them. Devour them. Make them mine.

I pinch my thigh. Enough.

"How are you feeling?" Lennox asks. His eyes are fixed on me, observing my every move. I wonder if he can sense my arousal. Ryker knew immediately, he could smell it, but Lennox is a wolf, he's not supposed to be interested in females of another species. That wouldn't be good for evolution after all.

"Good." They don't need to know the details. "How have you been?"

This is ridiculous. We're behaving like we're random friends meeting up after a long time. I should stop this, change it, but I don't know how. How do you behave after you've been brought back from the dead? How do you thank the people who helped you? How do you accept that you weren't able to save yourself, that you had to rely on others?

"Bored," Lennox says and pulls a crisp from one of Bethany's bags. The crunch of it disappearing into his mouth almost makes me jump up and shout something ridiculous like 'eat me instead'. Maybe I should go back upstairs and chain myself to my hammock. Not let myself be around men until it's all over.

"Me too." Gryphon finally leans back in his chair and crosses his arms behind his head. "I saw Little Kat earlier today though. She's happy with my aunt, but she asked for you. Don't suppose you want to accompany me there to see her?"

"Not today," I hedge. "There are other things I need to do."

Lennox perks up. "Like attacking the Pack and killing everyone?"

Despite myself, I have to laugh. "I take it that's on your to-do list?"

He nods enthusiastically. "But I'm not stupid enough to do it. We need to do something about them though. There have been reports of Pack shifters disappearing off the streets. Ryker has told us that his cats aren't seeing as many shifters as they used to. I think the Pack leaders are pulling everyone back to regroup, but I bet they're planning to go on the offensive soon."

"Then we have to be ready for that." I'm glad we've moved onto familiar territory again, although I can't help but look at his lips, wet from his tongue licking away some salty crisp crumbs. Ovaries, behave. I don't have time for this.

"Have you had time yet to look at the stuff we retrieved from their lab?" Gryphon asks.

I shake my head. "Bethany is looking at some cloning files she found, but that's all I know so far."

"I'll make some coffee," Lennox says with a sigh and gets up from the sofa. "This is going to take some time."

"Tea for me, with lots of milk."

He grins. "I know. Gryphon, how do you take it?"

The moment of truth. How a person takes their tea says a lot about them. Lots of sugar? Sweet and indulgent personality. Lots of milk? Probably some cat genes. Nothing at all? Boring, serious or psychopathic.

"Milk and sugar, but make the tea strong."

Mmhm, that's a hard one to interpret. Is that a siren thing or a Gryphon preference? I never had the chance to find out more about his kind. He's said sirens are in control of the Pack, but he seems to have an aunt here as well as a sister. Are they on our side? The Pack's? Neutral?

By now, I doubt he'd ever betray me, but I still need to find out his situation. Family can be one of the best ways to manipulate someone into doing your wishes. I've used that method often enough myself. Until now, I didn't have a family, but now I have Little Kat, and my employees, and maybe even these men. Just as friends, obviously, associates. Fucking Ryker was a mistake that was only down to my heat problem. And Lennox.... let's not think about that. He's not talked about me being his wolf's mate again, so I'd rather keep it like that. It's too complicated, too emotionally stressful.

"Penny for your thoughts?"

Gryphon's eyes roam my face. I keep my expression neutral. "Just thinking how quickly things have changed."

"Very true. Look at us, waiting for Lennox to make us tea. Never thought I'd ever be served by a wolf."

"Watch it!" Lennox shouts from the kitchen. "I'm not a service dog!"

I snicker. Lennox has always hated being called a dog, and now he's doing it himself. Things really have changed.

I turn to Gryphon. "Fill me in. What did you find? I need all the info you got."

"As I said, this is going to take a while. We've started going through the files we retrieved, but a lot of it is written in sciencey jargon and even your colleagues don't always know what it's supposed to mean."

I huff impatiently. "Enough of the preamble, start telling me the important stuff."

He smiles in amusement, but then his expression changes to something else, something darker. A shiver runs down my back at the intensity in his gaze. "Do you want the gentle or the brutal version?"

"What do you mean?"

"I can tell you the truth without making you feel bad. If I give you all the details, however, it might upset you. Some of the things we found in the lab aren't for the faint of heart."

"I'm definitely not faint of heart," I protest, but secretly I appreciate his warning. I'm a clone. I'm not really what I thought I was. There might be more of me, there might be answers I don't want to be true. But when have I ever retreated from a problem? Besides drowning my worries in catnip?

"Give me the full version. Don't try to protect me from the truth. I need to know."

He nods and clears his throat. "Alright then. You were the first clone, and the one who survived for the longest. Which is surprising, given how many they terminated because they weren't perfect enough. You'd think that the first would be the worst, in a way. The least perfected. Maybe they wanted you as a control subject to compare to future versions."

Coldness spreads through my veins and I want to make him stop talking, but I need to hear this. There's no hiding from the truth. Not knowing would be worse.

"How many?" I ask hoarsely.

"Counting the embryos that never came to full term, fifty-three."

I swallow hard. Fifty-three versions of me.

"Little Kat, she was called K8 by the woman in the lab. I thought there might only be eight of us," I whisper, unable to hide my emotions from Gryphon. The walls around me are crumbling.

"They only named the ones K plus a number who survived past their first year. You're K1, then there were six other children before Little Kat. There seems to have been two other girls after her, but I've not been able to find any information on their whereabouts. The children must have been kept somewhere else, not in the lab."

"They weren't at the Pack headquarters either. I lived there and never saw anyone who looked like me. I would have been able to smell them, their cat shifter scent, even if I hadn't recognised them for some reason. They must be in another building that we don't know about."

Gryphon nods. "We're going to find them, but they know now that we're onto them. They'll likely hide the clones, making it harder for us to seek them out."

"Children," I correct. "Not clones. Please."

He gives me a tight smile. "Of course. Children. According to the data, the youngest would be about three, and the oldest sixteen. Maybe we should focus on the oldest first. If they raised her similarly to you, she'd be out there, doing hits and working for the Pack."

I shake my head. "Unlikely. If she'd be running around town, I would have noticed, trust me."

"That means they either keep them locked inside or she's not in this town." He sighs. "I may be able to use some of my contacts to find out if there are any cat shifters in other cities controlled by my people, but that's going to be neither easy nor quick. I have to be careful, they cannot know that I'm working against them."

"Do it. We need to have a chat about your family at some point, but first, continue with what you found out."

Lennox uses that moment to return with a tray. He didn't just make tea, he also made some finger sandwiches. I'm keeping him. Service dog indeed.

I snatch a salmon sandwich and take a big bite. I've had a lot of catnip biscuits already, but they don't really sate my hunger, they just made me happier.

"Well done, mate," Gryphon mutters while chewing on a cherry tomato.

Mate? Are they that close now? Has Gryphon told the others about what he is?

"Go on," I remind him, ignoring that he's trying to eat.

"Alright. Seven children. We have Little Kat, so there's still a way to go. I think you should talk to her, make sure she doesn't know anything else that could help us. She's recovering well, getting some meat on her bones again, and she's getting better at having normal conversations."

I nod. "Can you take me to her later today?"

"Of course."

"Tell her about the doctor," Lennox encourages. "The woman we killed."

"Grandma Doctor. It's a pity we don't have her here for interrogation and a lot of torture, but that can't be helped. Lennox found some intelligence on her in the upstairs offices. She's been with the Pack since she finished university, recruited by a scientist called Professor Lakefield. Not sure if he's still alive or what's become of him, but he seems to have been the first to experiment with cloning. Grandma Doctor is actually called Jacqueline Fitzroy, she's got a PhD in genetics and wrote a couple of papers on human evolution. Of course nothing she has published mentions shifters, but she quit academia pretty quickly after she got involved with the Pack. Together with Lakefield, she researched how to make shifters stronger, while also removing some of their free will. They didn't have collars back when they started; shifters were controlled by blackmail, threats to their families and brainwashing. Inventing the collars made Fitzroy one of the most important people in the Pack. I've seen her bank accounts. She was probably the richest woman in town."

"We may have syphoned off some of that money," Lennox adds with a chuckle. "Before they realised that she's dead."

Good. It's not really making me feel better about what that woman has done, but at least she'll keep Meow running for a bit longer. And it would be kind of ironic if we used her money to bring the Pack down.

"So she invented the collars and started the cloning experiments?" I clarify.

"Yes. Once she'd got a working prototype of the collar, she realised that while it helped control shifters, it didn't work when they were in their animal forms. She basically had stronger humans with the collars, but she wouldn't be able to get them to do their bidding when shifted. That's when she started thinking about other ways to control shifters, starting at the very beginning of their life. Cloning the strongest, then adjusting their free will and obedience levels. That was her aim, creating an obedient shifter who had great intelligence but obeyed every single command."

I shiver at the thought. Being forced to do someone's bidding without even knowing that it's wrong, without having the choice to resist... I can imagine nothing worse. They tried to control me all my life, but I fought back, didn't let them turn me into their slave, even though my resistance was often painful. Yes, in the end, I always did what they told me to, but on my own terms. The times when I secretly spent time with Lennox under the bridge, when we stole away to the market to steal some sweets, those were the moments I truly felt like myself. That doctor tried to take that away from other children like me. If she wasn't already dead, I'd make sure that she'd die a horrible, painful death. Preferably with a collar around her neck, as a reminder for what she's done to others.

"Are you okay?" Lennox asks softly and I realise that I've balled my fists, squashing my sandwich into mush. I force myself to relax and nod, putting on a brave face.

"Did they succeed?" I ask, dreading the answer. "Little Kat wasn't under their control once we took off the collar, so they hadn't got there by the time they created her. What if they managed to succeed with the final two?"

"I don't know," Gryphon says quietly, looking at the sandwich in his hands. He's not taken a bite yet, waiting for the story to be over. "We didn't find anything about them, not a single file. It's as if they made sure that everything about those two children was kept secret. Maybe that means they succeeded. Maybe not. Who knows, and we can't exactly ask her or any of the other people in the lab. They're all dead." He sighs. "If that Professor is still alive, he'd be well into his eighties by now, but it's worth a try."

"I'm already on it," Lennox interjects.

"Don't you have to work for your employer still?" I ask him. "Or are you with us the whole time now?"

He quirks an eyebrow. "Would you like me to leave?"

I quickly shake my head, the thought of him being gone making me strangely anxious. It must be the heat thing, it's making me all emotional. I can't work like this. I need my emotions to stay in check, but right now, they're all over the place.

"I've asked for some time off. Surprisingly, they said yes. I doubt they're going to leave me be for long though, so I'm kind of expecting them to give me a new order any day now. Still, I'll try and help out as much as I can."

I meet his eyes, realising how much regret he's

hiding. "If you wanted, could you leave?" I ask gently. "Would they let you go for good?"

He looks away. "I'm not sure. I've not been brave enough to find out yet."

I'll add that to my list. Making sure Lennox can leave his employers, whoever they may be, preferably to join Meow. And me.

No, stop it, heated ovaries. Not me. Just Meow.

CHAPTER FIVE

As soon as Gryphon and I are out of the door, I ask him about his family.

"How is it that your aunt and sister are here, but you've said you've left your family?"

"My sister left before me, officially to go to university. She only stayed for the first semester, then decided she wanted to become an artist. It was a clever plan, really. My dad disowned her and sent her away. Now, she's got as much freedom as she wants and doesn't even have to pretend to be something she's not."

He sounds a little bitter. "Why didn't you do the same?"

"The siren community is very traditional. Men are in charge. If I'd tried to leave, it would have been a public embarrassment for my father, so he'd probably have killed me and pretended I'd died from natural causes. My sister was never intended to have a role of authority anyway, so losing her wasn't such a big deal."

"Was it the same with her aunt?"

"Not quite. She was a big believer in my family's cause until her husband died. That completely changed her. I've been told she went crazy for months, totally unstable and unpredictable. Since her husband had been an important man, they didn't get rid of her, but gave her a little house and a pension far away from where she could give them any embarrassment or trouble. To be honest, I'm still not sure if she pretended to be crazy so that she could get away or if she actually was. Nowadays, she's as sane as you and me."

I chuckle. "Are you saying I'm sane?"

"Apologies, of course not." He grins. "How could I ever insinuate such a thing."

We walk on in silence. It's strange not running over rooftops but actually walking along the streets like normal people. The town is quite busy, but both of us are experts in avoiding bumping into people. The only times I do that is to pick their pockets, but I haven't done that in a while. I used to love the thrill of robbing people without them realising, but then I learned how to kill and decided I liked that a lot more.

Gryphon leads me into one of the wealthier parts of town. Nice of his people to give his aunt a house in this area. Maybe they tried to pay her off, make her feel in their debt.

Before we can even get to the house, a flash of red hair comes running from the side and suddenly, I'm being hugged. I look down at Little Kat who's got her arms around my waist, her head pressed against my belly. Okay then. I don't think I've ever been hugged by a child.

Gryphon laughs and I smoothen my surprised expression. He doesn't need to know how both weird and good this feels.

"It's good to see you, Katriona," the little girl squeals.

"Kat," I correct her.

She shakes her head, still hugging me tightly. "I'm Kat, so you can't be Kat too."

Gryphon bends over with laughter while I glare at him.

"I was there first," I tell her sternly. "If anyone needs to change their name, it's you."

"You're older, you almost look like a Katriona."

I stare at her. "Did you just call me old?"

She steps back and shrugs with a wide smile. "You're definitely older than me, which makes you old because I'm young."

The logic of insolent children. Gryphon is choking, laughing hard, but I ignore him. Otherwise I'd have to kill him.

"Are you feeling better?" the girl asks, looking up and down my body as if she's trying to see an injury that prevented me from visiting her before.

"Yes, everything's back to normal." Almost. The urge to jump Gryphon isn't quite normal. Even the thought makes heat pool in my core, but no, that's entirely inappropriate, not just because Little Kat is watching me closely.

"Good. Then you can help me."

"Help you with what?"

"Becoming like you."

Gryphon had just stopped laughing, but now he explodes into chuckles once again. We both ignore him.

"Why do you want to be like me?" I ask, genuinely astonished. There's nothing about me that should appeal to a little girl. I'm an assassin, I kill people. I don't have a social life, I'm not pretty, I don't own a lot of nice things. I'm not particularly friendly, I enjoy being rude and I'm... well, I wouldn't want to be like me most of the time.

"You're strong," she says simply. "You can kill them all. I'm not strong enough yet."

Oh my. She really is my clone. A little baby assassin.

"Who do you want to kill?" I question her, keeping my tone neutral.

"Everyone. All the people who hurt me. Who hurt you. Who're hurting others."

"The Pack?"

"Yes, and the others who came to see me."

That makes me kneel down in front of her so that I can look in her eyes. "What others?"

"I don't know, but they weren't human. They smelled different, nothing I've ever come across. They watched me during the tests."

Gryphon stops laughing and comes closer. "Did they smell like me?"

She shakes her head. "No, not like you. Some of the people in the Pack smell like you, but not the visitors. They were different."

I meet Gryphon's eyes, exchanging a look. A different species, neither shifter nor siren. Little Kat has met Lily, so it can't have been succubi either or she would have made the connection. What else was there? Until I met Lily, I'd only ever been around humans and shifters.

"Did they look human?" I ask and Little Kat nods.

"But they smelled different, sweet. Like they'd taste good if you started to eat them."

Okay, call me shocked. Is she actually talking about eating people? Please don't let her be a cannibal.

Gryphon clears his throat. "Have you ever eaten someone?"

She looks up at him. "Of course not, but sometimes they gave me blood to drink. It can taste really yucky but there is also blood that is good."

Bile rises up in my throat. They made her drink blood. That's just wrong. Yes, sometimes when I'm shifted and kill someone, I may have accidentally swallowed some blood, but I'd never drink it like a vampire. So wrong.

"Well, we're not going to give you blood," I tell her with a forced smile. "Has Gryphon's aunt been feeding you well?"

She nods enthusiastically. "She's made pancakes for me every evening. With lots of chocolate sauce."

Now that sounds more like me. I wonder if there are any left, or if the woman will make some tonight. I could stay for a bit... pancakes are life.

I stand up straight and Little Kat immediately takes my hand. First hugging, now handholding. Next she'll want to sleep in my bed and demand bedtime stories. I need to make it very clear to her that I'm not her mother. I might be something of her sister, kind of, but I'm not made out to be her carer. I hope she can stay with Gryphon's aunt for a while longer. Permanently, maybe. Give her a chance of a normal life.

"Come in or the ice cream will melt!" a woman shouts through the open window.

Ice cream? The cat in me meows loudly.

Gryphon shoots me a look.

Oh. I actually meowed. Seems I'm not quite back to normal after all.

AUNT ROSE IS A VOLUPTUOUS, GLOWING WOMAN WITH twinkling eyes and hair so full of volume that it seems to have a life of its own. It seems to move without her moving, without there being any wind.

She's sat us down around her kitchen table and put a bowl of ice cream and strawberries in front of us. There's even some whipped cream on the top. I like her already.

"Tuck in," she says with a wide smile. "Don't let it melt."

Little Kat immediately starts shovelling ice cream into her mouth, seemingly unconcerned by how cold it is. I'm a little slower, forcing myself to savour every bite.

"Amazing," Gryphon sighs. "Remind me to visit more often."

Rose chuckles. "If I can lure you here with ice cream, so be it."

"And strawberries," he hastens to add. "Those are kind of essential."

"Obviously. Usually you'd get a chocolate flake too but Kat has eaten them all."

I'm about to protest that I've done no such thing before remembering that I'm not the only Kat in the room. This really is getting confusing, but I'm not going to be the one to change her name. Little Kat could always come up with something unique, something that's hers. Maybe that's the angle I should take. Tell her that to be like me, she needs to be her own person, with her own name. Yes, that's going to be the plan from now on.

"It's nice to finally meet you," Rose says once all our bowls have been licked clean. In Little Kat's case, that is. I'm jealous that she's still a child and allowed to do that. At home, if I were alone, I'd definitely lick it clean myself, but I'm pretending to be a grown-up just now.

"Nice to meet you too."

That's about as far as my manners and knowledge of small talk go. Let's hope she won't start talking about the weather.

"Is Y around?" Gryphon asks. "I've not seen her in a while."

His aunt snorts. "Neither have I. She's with that boy again. Young love."

His eyes widen. "My sister has a boyfriend?"

"Oh, I thought you knew. Well, she's going to kill me for telling you, but yes, it's been going on for a couple of weeks now. She's hardly ever here, spending all her time at his place. I remember how I was when I first met Jimmy. Just the same, always together every minute of the day, as if being apart was a waste of time. You should ask her to introduce him to you. I've not met him yet but he sounds lovely."

"She says he's goooorgeous," Little Kat adds. "She always draws out the O when she talks about him. Gooooorgeous."

Seeing her act like this, happy and innocent, makes me happier than I thought it would. It means there's hope for her. She may have had a crappy start to life, but that might not mean that she can't ever be happy. Maybe, with time, she'll be able to forget her past and start anew. And I'm going to help her with that. It's too late for me to forget what the Pack has done to me, but she still has a chance.

"Now I definitely want to meet him." Gryphon doesn't look happy. Is he a protective older brother? Or is he a controlling one? A jealous one?

"Are you going to stay for dinner?" Rose asks.

Before I can ask if there will be pancakes, Gryphon shakes his head. "We've got some things to do, but thanks for the offer."

"Can I come?" Little Kat looks at me expectantly.

"I'm afraid not, but before we go, I need to have a chat with you. Maybe somewhere private?"

Rose shoots me a curious glance but then nods and leads us to a small sitting room. Probably not the only living room in this house. It's too big and fancy for that. This might be a sort of waiting chamber, or a place to have a drink before the main meal. Who knows, it's not like I know posh stuff like that.

"When can I come home with you?" Little Kat asks

as soon as we've sat down on a plump yellow sofa. Not a colour I would have chosen.

I find it interesting how she calls it home already. She was at the Meow headquarters for what, one day? Two days? And now she calls it her home. Children are weird.

"For now, it's best you stay here. The Pack will retaliate and they might come to attack Meow. If that happens, I want you as far away from danger as possible. They don't know you're here, which means you're safe."

"I'd be safe with you," she complains. "You'd keep me safe."

I'm struck by the faith she has in me. Is it just because I'm her clone, her older sister?

"I'd try my hardest to keep you safe," I reassure her, "but we're outnumbered if the Pack decides to go on the offensive. You understand that, right?"

She meets my eyes and after a moment's hesitation, she nods.

I smile at her. "It sounds like it's pretty good living here with Rose. Pancakes and ice cream, I'm almost tempted to move here myself."

Little Kat laughs and licks her lips. "Auntie Rose is a great cook. She's reading stories to me too, every evening."

"That's nice of her. What kind of stories?"

"Stuff about princes and dragons and evil witches. I keep telling her that nothing in those books is true but she says that's the point."

I can't help but chuckle. Little Kat is not used to fairy tales. Of course, neither am I, nor would I have been at her age. There were no bedtime stories at the Pack. I sometimes stole a book from one of my victims so that I could train my reading skills, but most of those were adult books, nothing about princes.

"Enjoy it," I tell her. "You've had a hard time, let's just enjoy all the good things happening to you now."

She nods, her expression serious as if I've given her an order that she intends to follow. "But I can come and live with you soon?"

"Once the danger is over, we can talk about that again."

Disappointment spreads across her face. She's not learned yet how to hide her feelings.

"Just because I need to find a nice room for you," I quickly add and her mouth curves into a small smile. "And get everything you need. I've never had a child stay with me before."

I almost expected her to protest at me calling her a child, but she stays quiet.

"Now, before I go, I need to ask you a few questions. It's very important that you try and answer them, okay?"

She nods, all business again.

"When you were with Grandma Doctor, did you ever see other children?"

She frowns and her eyes turn glassy, like she's looking inside her mind, searching for memories.

"Maybe," she whispers after a long while. "I heard them talking about others, but I'm not sure if I ever met one. It's hard to remember, I was wearing the collar."

She rubs her throat and my own hand immediately

goes to clutch my neck. We're both damaged. Hopefully, she'll be able to get over it. She's still young.

"Were there any people with our hair colour? That's hard to miss." I give her a little smile. Her hair is as fiery as mine, although it seems smoother.

She frowns, looking into the distance. "Once... a woman, maybe as old as you. She was on a chair next to me. She didn't speak to me, just looked at me for a long time. Then they made us both sleep and when I woke up, she was gone."

I clench my fists. That might have been the clone after me, the one who'd be sixteen right now. For Little Kat, she might have looked old. The alternative, her being a clone we don't know about, is one I choose to ignore.

"I'm sorry," she sniffs. "It's hard to remember. It's like there's fog everywhere and I'm afraid I'll get lost if I walk in too far."

I take her hand and give it a squeeze in what I hope is a reassuring gesture. I've seen other people do it. "That's fine. We'll figure it out, don't worry. If you remember anything else, let me know. Aunt Rose knows how to contact me. And maybe write it down too so you don't forget."

Her eyes widen. "I don't know how to."

"How to do what?"

Her lips quiver and she looks away. "Write."

Oh my. They never taught her. Fuckers.

"Do you know how to read though?"

She nods eagerly. "A little."

"Good, that's good. I'll talk to Rose, maybe she can

help you with learning how to write. Would you like that?"

Her nodding becomes ecstatic.

I give her a wide smile, trying to hide my sadness. "Once this is all over, we might even be able to send you to school. You could meet other children your age, make friends, learn how to read and write and all sorts of other things."

"Really?"

"Really. But first we need to deal with the Pack. It's not safe for any of us while they're still in charge."

She bites her lower lip, then meets my eyes. "There's one thing I remembered."

"Yes?"

"They took me to a house. A blue house with a red roof. I don't want to remember what they did there but maybe you can find the house. It was big."

I flinch at the pain in her eyes. No child should ever have to feel this amount of pain.

CHAPTER SIX

We're quiet on our way back home. Gryphon hasn't asked what Little Kat told me, and while I will fill him in eventually, I first need to get over the fact of how much they mistreated her. I knew that, of course, from seeing the state she was in when we first found her. But seeing the pain in her eyes, the desperate attempt not to remember some of the things she went through... it hurts.

I always thought I had it bad, but it turns out I basically had the perfect childhood compared to her.

I need to distract myself from those gloomy thoughts. I need my brain functional and rational.

"Your aunt is nice," I say randomly.

"She is. Wait until you taste her pancakes."

"Is she all about food?"

He shrugs. "She doesn't talk much about her life before her husband died. So yes, it's all about food with her. She loves to chat about what's going on in town, what gossip she knows, what book she's just read, but she never mentions the past. It's like she forces herself to live in the present. Maybe she's afraid she might go crazy again if she dwells on her past for too long."

"That makes sense." I stop and he looks at me questioningly. "We need to talk. If we go against the Pack, that also means we're going against your family. You might have escaped their notice during our attack on their lab, but if we do a full assault on their headquarters, I doubt they won't realise your involvement."

He nods. "I know."

"You said your father would kill you if you defied him."

Gryphon shrugs. "Yes. He can try. But if there's no Pack, that also means he has no influence over this town any longer. He'd have to physically come here, or send someone to do it for him. I know the way he thinks, I'll be able to evade him. And if it comes to it, I will kill him myself."

There's steel in his voice, metal that has been forged long ago. He's ready to do it, if he has to.

"I'll help you. You've fought on my side and I will be on yours."

He steps closer, bridging the distance between us. My skin tickles at his closeness.

"I appreciate that." His voice has changed, turning hoarse and deep.

It totally turns me on. If we weren't surrounded by people, I'd jump him. I'm so tempted to slip my hands underneath his shirt, to take him where we are, to fuck him like it's the end of the world.

"Kat."

His voice is honey and catnip, luring me towards him. My lips are on his before I can stop myself, and then we're kissing, hard and wild, our tongues dancing, our breaths mingling. Burning desire spreads through me. If I don't take him now, something is going to happen. I'm close to exploding, full of energy that needs to be used.

I barely feel the sting of pain as my fingernails turn to claws. I rake them over his back and he groans, pulling me against his chest, his mouth ravaging mine.

"Get a room!" someone shouts and just like that, I'm ripped from my sexual frenzy. I step back, the heat in my body disappearing quickly, giving way to a twinge of embarrassment. Damn Kat-in-heat. I don't fuck men I know. At least I didn't use to. I had a clear code of satisfying my needs without ever getting attached. Now I just snogged a guy in the middle of a busy street, not caring that he's a friend, someone who's hopefully going to stick around. I can't have that jeopardised by my own misguided hormones.

Gryphon clears his throat. "How about we go to my place? It's not far."

He's got a place? Yes, I want to scream, take me home so we can continue this, but rational Kat takes over.

"We should go back and make plans."

I expect him to nod and accept that, but no, he wraps his arms around my waist once more and pulls me close.

"I don't think so, Kat. You've woken the siren and you better finish what you started."

His eyes are green pools of desire, shimmering unnaturally. Is that the siren in him? Is there a physical change or did he just speak metaphorically?

"My place, now, before I take you here and now."

His voice is a husky whisper, and just like that, the heat is back, and with it, the urge to have him deep inside of me. Fuck rational Kat.

I let him take my hand and lead me away from the crowds. Through narrow streets we go, almost running, both of us desperate to fulfil our urges.

"If we're not there any time soon..." I threaten, my claws coming out once more. Letting him take me against a wall of a random house doesn't sound too bad just now. My blood is boiling, my body screaming for release. I need him, need him so much.

I don't care that I've only just been with Ryker. And that I was with Lennox not too long ago. Right now, my cat senses are taking over, and cats take multiple mates. I no longer care about human conventions. I want what is mine, and Gryphon is a prize that I'm going to claim.

"Almost there."

He's out of breath; not sure if it's from running or suppressing his siren needs. I've never been with a siren before. Is it going to be different? Is he different, anatomically? Am I going to be surprised when I rip his black leather trousers off his body?

A large tenement block looms over us, dark and brooding. Not a place I'd like to live in, but Gryphon pulls me through the front door, up two flights of stairs and then we're in his flat. We never make it to his bedroom.

His clothes end up in a shrivelled mess on the ground, and then he's naked, gloriously naked in front of me. I let him keep his boots, and somehow the look of him in his high leather boots and nothing else turns me on even more. A primal desire makes me growl and push him against the wall.

I put a hand around his throat, pinning him in place, and ravage his mouth, soaking him in, claiming him as mine. I thought the kiss in the street was wild, but this is something else. He gasps for air, and I realise I'm squeezing his throat too tightly. I lessen the pressure a little and he sucks in a deep breath. His eyes are fixed on mine, never wavering, never letting me out of his sight.

And then he begins to sing.

His voice is full-bodied like a cask of aged whisky, laced with honey, smooth like silk. His song wraps around me, hugging me tight, roaming over my body like a hundred hands.

I step away from him, completely trapped in his enchantment. I take off my clothes, because the song tells me to, and present myself to him, my siren. His music caresses my body, touches me, makes me quiver.

Gryphon stands there, his hands around his cock, singing while his eyes roam my body, watching as his song prepares me for him. My nipples become hard and perky as the invisible force wraps around my breasts. I moan, my hands desperate to touch something, to hold onto someone, but Gryphon is too far away. He must know what I need yet he revels in his power, in his control.

The music fills my head, shows me images of him and me, entwined, connected, as one. I touch myself, rub my core, because that's what the song tells me to do. Maybe I could fight it, perhaps I could break the spell and run, but why would I? This is precisely what I want and need.

Guided by the music, I step back until my naked back is against the wall, and spread my legs. Finally, Gryphon moves, walks towards me, his cock hard and ready, and then he's finally inside me, filling me all the way. The song turns wild and we fuck like animals, my claws breaking his skin, his teeth sinking into my neck while he pushes into me with fervour, making me moan with every thrust. We're no longer human, nor are we pretending to be. We are creatures of the night, made to follow our instincts, and the moment I realise that is the moment I let go.

Nothing matters but him. His touch. His song. His body against mine. Our dance, to music he creates, a melody that is ours alone, born by the wildness in our hearts.

MY BODY IS SORE WHEN I SLOWLY RESURFACE FROM THE pure need controlling my mind. We're on Gryphon's bed which is too small for both of us, which is why I'm half on top of him, one of my legs dangling in the air. We've had a shower, then ended up on the rug in the living room, then on the bed, then another shower, now we're back on the bed, but the lust racing through my veins is finally dissipating. My muscles are aching from all sorts of strange positions that Gryphon's siren voice made us try. I'm not sure how much control he had about it all.

There are no regrets, though. It was worth the soreness.

I lick my lips, thirsting for some water, but getting up from the bed seems like too much of an effort. Instead, I rest on his chest, listening to his steady heartbeat.

"Thank you," he whispers.

I blink open an eye. "Why?"

"For accepting the siren. For not running away."

I smile happily. "It was far too good to run away."

He stretches his arms, banging his wrists against the wall. This room is entirely too small for two people. The entire flat is tiny, but I guess it's enough for only one person. I've not seen the kitchen yet, but I hope he's got his fridge stocked with junk food. I never eat healthy after sex. My body needs lots of calories to stock up with energy.

"I can't do that with humans," he says quietly. I can't see his face, but I can hear the regret in his voice. "They usually end up dead. The siren is too strong."

"They die from sex?" I ask incredulously.

"No, from the energy the siren pulls from them. A bit like what succubi do, except that it doesn't have to be sex for the siren. It can feast on fear too. On most emotions, actually, but most people in my family prefer fear." He laughs coldly. "One of the many reasons why I left."

"So.... does that mean you fed from me?"

He slips his hand under my chin and lifts my head, forcing me to look at him. "You didn't realise?"

"No."

"But...you don't feel exhausted now? Drained?"

"Yes, but that's normal after what we've just done. I don't feel more tired than I should."

He frowns, still holding my head in place. "Strange, I feel like the siren has fed. It's content and relaxed. I've not felt this free in ages."

"You talk as if your siren is separate of you. I thought you were a siren?"

He grimaces. "I'm called a siren, that's my species, but I'm something in between while my siren part resides deep within me. Maybe it's me, maybe this is just a protective mechanism that I've developed to tell myself that it's not me doing all those things. But yes, it's separate, and I can control it most of the time, but when it hasn't fed for a while, it gets harder for me to control. Out there in the street, when you tempted me, I almost lost control. They only way I got it back for a while was promising the siren that I would bring you here. So that we could have you." He gently lowers my head to his chest again, probably so that he doesn't have to look at me anymore. I still saw the shame in his eyes, just for a second. He's blaming himself for something that didn't happen.

"You didn't feed on me. I promise you that if I had wanted, I could have fought against the siren's song, but I didn't want to. I needed you as much as you needed me."

He chuckles sadly. "I somehow doubt that."

I take a deep breath, already regretting what I'm about to say. "I'm in heat. Like a cat. Well, I am a cat, so I guess I'm a cat in heat. Except that this has never happened before and I feel like jumping everyone and now after I've been with you it all feels so much better."

The words ramble from my lips. My thoughts are all over the place. I shouldn't have told him. It's too embarrassing. Too revealing. Never tell others what they don't need to know. That used to be my rule. Don't expose yourself. Don't show them what you feel, what you think.

I'm no longer strong enough to live by those rules. I've become weak. Emotional. Human. What I need is to run around as a cat for a couple of days to fight my humanity. Then stay away from Gryphon, Ryker and Lennox. And the other Meow people. I've become far too close to them. It's distracting me from what's really important.

"You're in heat," Gryphon repeats. "Are you going to hump my leg anytime soon? Should I be worried that you might pee on my shoes?"

I sit up and look at him, half angry, half amused.

"My cat used to do that," he explains with a wry smile. "Sat on my favourite shoes and literally filled them with her pee. You can't imagine what a relief it was when we had her spayed."

I stiffen.

His smile grows wider. "Don't worry, I have no intentions of having you spayed. Although I'm sorry, the siren never thinks about things like protection. Do you... could you get pregnant?"

I stare at him in surprise. I'd not thought of that.

"I doubt it. Maybe if I slept with another cat shifter, but..."

Fuck.

CHAPTER SEVEN

If there is a pregnancy test for cats, I've never seen one before. Instead, I pop by the pharmacy and get myself some morning-after pills. They're for humans, but in the end, it would be human me giving birth, not cat me. At least I've never heard of a shifter whose animal form got pregnant. That would be... well, who am I to judge.

By the time we're back at the Meow headquarters, my earlier happiness has slowly given way to the same familiar urge as before. I think it's getting worse. I already feel ready to fuck someone again. This can't continue like that. I'm not that kind of person. There's far too much work to do and I cannot neglect Meow because of my stupid hormone issue.

"You've been gone for a while!" Lily shouts from upstairs as soon as I step foot inside. "Is Gryphon with you?"

"Yes," he calls back, giving me a questioning look. I shrug. No idea what Lily wants him for.

"Kat?"

This time it's Bethany shouting from the lab below us.

I sigh. "Why does everyone want stuff from me?"

Gryphon laughs. "That's why I'm a freelancer. I have no idea how you do it, being responsible for other people besides yourself."

"Trust me, most days I regret it."

I sigh again and head downstairs, deciding that Beth might have a more exciting and urgent problem for me to solve. After all, she was working on the cloning experiments the Pack have done.

She meets me at the door to her lab, already taken off her coat.

"Is Ryker there?" she asks.

"No idea, I only just came home. Why?"

"I tested Pumpkin's DNA. I think I should tell him first."

I nod. "Is it good news?"

"Depends on whether you want Pumpkin to be a shifter or not. But I also found some interesting stuff about your cl... siblings."

"What?"

Both nervousness and excitement rise up in me.

"I know what happened to at least two of them."

I stare at her in surprise, then grab her by the shoulders.

"Tell me. Now."

"They were sold."

Pieces of me shatter. Sold. Like livestock. Like slaves.

"Where? When?" I whisper, desperately trying to stay in control.

"A couple of years ago. K4 and K5."

"Who did they sell them to?"

Even asking that question leaves a bitter taste in my mouth.

"Stormborough, according to the records. They're twins and were sold to something or someone called Trauerstein. I'm afraid that's all I can tell you, all I have is an invoice."

She swallows hard, sharing my pain.

An invoice. Like you use for goods being sold. Not children. Not girls exactly like me. I'm beginning to think that I had it the best out of all ten of us. I got out of it alive without being permanently harmed. Now I have a life, I make my own decisions, I'm my own woman. I'm free. My siblings though, who knows how many of them are even still alive. Forty-three of us never survived past our first year of life. It's all so wrong.

"I've never heard of anyone called Trauerstein. Maybe it's an organisation like the Pack. I'll ask the others, one of them might know."

I turn and walk away from her, hiding my face. I don't want her to see that I'm about to cry.

CATS DON'T CRY. HUMANS DO. RIGHT NOW, I'M AS human as they come, locked inside the bathroom, trying to stem the flow of tears. Maybe it's the imbalance of hormones raging within me. Maybe it's because I'm sad.

Before I met Little Kat, I never knew that there were more of me. Now that I do, it scares me to bits that not all of us might still be alive.

"Kat?"

Halfway up the stairs, Ryker corners me. I hadn't even realised he was in the house. He's holding little Pumpkin in his arms, his muscles bulging around the little kitten. Pumpkin happily meows at me. He has no idea about what's going on. I wish I could say the same.

I wipe my eyes, making sure no treacherous tears show.

"What's wrong?" Ryker asks, running his eyes over me as if he's looking for injuries. No, he can't see my wounds, those are deep inside; scratches on my heart, bleeding gashes that won't ever heal.

"I'll tell you later."

My voice is choked and brittle. Better if I don't talk too much right now. I don't want him to see how weak I feel just now.

"Alright, I'll hold you to that. Lily told me that Bethany has got the results of Pumpkin's blood test." He ruffles his son's fur. "Want to come and find out what he is?"

Going back to the lab? Facing Beth again, being reminded of what she just told me?

"No, you go, I think it's better if you do that on your own."

Disappointment flicks over his face, but it disappears quickly, pushed away by concern.

"Sure you're alright?"

I shrug. "Go, talk to Bethany."

I think if he didn't have an impatient Pumpkin is his arms, he'd stay and interrogate me, but luckily, the kitten meows loudly and Ryker walks away with a sigh.

Finally alone.

I slowly walk up the stairs, heading to my bedroom. My hammock and a thick blanket sound just like what I need right now. Hiding from this cruel, terrible world.

"Kat?"

I whirl around, glaring at Lennox. Why can't they all just leave me alone? "What?" I snarl.

"Nothing," he stutters, taken aback by my anger. "Is something wrong?"

I look at him. Seriously?

And then I start laughing. He's asking me if something's wrong. Hilarious.

Choked laughter turns into hysterical giggles. Lennox looks at me helplessly, but then I'm in his arms and he's holding me tight, his arms wrapped around me like the blanket I'm craving. I freeze, my laughter stops. I should run. Hide. Get away from him. I don't want him to see me like this.

But then he rubs my back and I let go. Tears drop onto his shirt, the wet evidence of my pain. I'd much prefer being wounded. An injury leaking blood is so much easier to deal with than my eyes pouring with tears.

His hands draw gentle circles on my back, forcing me to relax into him. I let him pull me close, let him hold me, almost afraid that he might push me away any second now. He doesn't know this Kat. I've always been strong around him. Now, I'm not. I'm the opposite.

Broken, sad, desperate for warmth. I need someone to tell me that everything will be alright, that my world will become a better place than it is now, but of course, I can't ask him to do that.

And I don't need to.

"Everything will be okay," he whispers softly as if he's read my thoughts. That makes even more tears quell from my eyes. "We'll find a way to get through this, Kat. You always survive, and you will this time, too. We'll get out at the other end and we'll be better for it."

I'm not quite sure what he means, but I let him soothe me with his whispered words, soaking them in like sun on a rainy day.

He shifts a little and I cling to him, scared that he'll leave.

"Don't worry," he whispers, "I'm just taking you somewhere more comfortable."

He lifts me into his arms, holding me against his chest, cradling me like a child. The normal Kat would kill him for that, but she's gone, her place taken by me, the weak, vulnerable Kat. I let him carry me into the living room. He sits me down on the sofa, gently touching my head, and walks away, locking the doors from the inside. That's Lennox, always aware of everyone's needs. He knows I don't want anyone to see me like this, so he's making sure that nobody will.

He returns to me, sits down by my side and wraps me in his arms once more. My tears are still flowing but my sobs are getting less. Him being here with me is helping. He grounds me, makes me feel safe.

I close my eyes and lean into him, letting him stroke my hair and rub my back. With every touch, I calm down a little until I blink away the final tear. Still, I don't move. I don't want to break this moment. I've never felt so happy to have Lennox with me. He's just what I need. He's reliable, dependable, and, even though we've been apart for a decade, I know I can trust him. He won't exploit my weakness. No, he'll help make me better, just like I would do the same for him. We're friends and we always will be.

PUMPKIN IS SETTLED ON MY LAP, SNORING SOFTLY. HE doesn't seem to care much about his DNA results, but his father is antsy, pacing the room while the rest of us are strewn all over the sofas. I'm leaning against Lennox's shoulder, but nobody has commented on that so far. Not Ryker, who I slept with on the attic floor, not Gryphon, who I fucked like an animal in his flat. There's no jealousy in their eyes. Surprising. Maybe I've misinterpreted their intentions. Or maybe they're simply all self-confident enough not to doubt that I care for others more than I care for them.

Lily has made us some hot chocolate - well, I think she's mostly made it for me after seeing my red-rimmed eyes and puffy nose - and Bethany has donated some of her favourite chocolate biscuits. Ben is noisily munching on two of them at once, interrupting the silence that has fallen over the room.

Ryker finally stops pacing and comes to a stop

behind the sofa opposite me. His eyes are wild, even more feline than they usually look.

"Pumpkin isn't a full shifter," he says abruptly, drawing all eyes to him. "But he's also not quite a cat, according to Bethany's results."

He runs a hand through his hair, obviously at a loss of what to do. I'd hoped he'd get a definite answer with the DNA test, but it seems it only made things even more confusing.

"It's possible that the shifter gene is dormant within Pumpkin," Bethany explains. "I'm not sure if it's strong enough to let him shift fully, but it might be years until we know for sure. Right now, he's mostly cat."

"I think he understands us humans better than other cats do," Benjamin says hesitantly. "When I talk to him, I feel like he actually understands every single word. The other cats mostly respond to my body language, but it's different with Pumpkin. Maybe that's because of his parentage."

Ryker nods. "Maybe. He's always been very clever for a kitten, but I always put it down to his upbringing. I've put a lot of effort into teaching him, into creating the nursery for all the kittens. Not all parents have the time or means to do that."

Pumpkin sneezes suddenly, his entire body shaking, but he's still asleep. I smile down at him, envying how he can just sleep through all the problems we're having to deal with.

"I guess we can't do anything but wait and see what he grows up to be," I mutter, tempted to pet the little kitten, but I don't want to wake him. He deserves a nap.

"Most of the pups of humans and wolf shifters turn out to be human with a bit of a temper," Lennox says, eyeing Pumpkin curiously. "But cats and wolves aren't alike in a lot of things, so who knows."

Ryker nods. "We shall see. I'm going to make sure he has a lot of contact with humans so that if he turns out to be a shifter, he'll already know their behaviour and will be able to fit in."

Not if he had the same eye colour as Ryker. I don't voice that thought though, I don't want to give him more worries than he already has. Ryker will never pass as a human, not with those glowing eyes. Gorgeous eyes that are now fixed on me. I melt in their honey shades, my hormones awakening once more. Not again.

He raises an eyebrow. Damn, he must be able to smell my arousal. How am I going to keep sane around him? At least the other two seem to be oblivious to the way my core throbs and my breasts press against the fabric of my shirt.

I need to do some research, maybe I'll find a solution to my little predicament. I can't stand this for much longer. If this was to go on for a few more days, weeks even... I'd die of embarrassment. I should probably leave and stay in a hermitage for a while, away from temptation. Away from men who look at me like Ryker does now.

"What are we going to do about the Pack?" Lennox asks. I'm grateful for the distraction.

I turn to him, hoping that Ryker is no longer staring at me. "I think my siblings have to be the priority for now. I know all shifters are suffering under the Pack's rule, but looking at the evidence we have, my siblings are being experimented on, tortured, mistreated. And now that the Pack knows that I'm aware of them, they might use the girls as leverage against me. They might even have brainwashed them enough that they can be sent as assassins. I'm not sure I could kill them even if I had to."

I swallow hard at the thought. Even when I wasn't sure if Little Kat was a trap sent by the Pack, I wouldn't have been able to harm her. The oldest of my siblings is around sixteen, which means she's still a child. And I don't hurt children. Ever.

Gryphon nods. "I agree. Having spent time with Little Kat, I can't even try to imagine what she's gone through. If the others are still alive, we need to find and free them."

Lennox looks like he's about to protest, but he stays quiet. He's been part of the Pack, so of course, he must see that as his priority.

"Rescuing the girls will be a blow for the Pack," I say, mostly to him. "They've created them as their weapons, so hopefully losing them will disrupt their plans of whatever it is they're hoping to achieve."

Slowly, he inclines his head. "I know, it's just that I've waited so long to move against the Pack and now that we might have the opportunity... but I get it, and I agree. First the girls, then we'll destroy the Pack once and for all."

He makes it sound so easy. I wish it was.

"There are ten of us," I summarise. "That means eight are still out there. Two of them have been... sold to someone in Stormborough. Do any of you have contacts there?"

To my surprise, Lily raises her hand. "My sister goes to the succubus academy there. I'll give her a call."

"Thanks, Beth can tell you more details."

I can't. I won't. Even telling them that two of my siblings have been sold like slaves has made me feel sick.

Lennox puts an arm around me and draws me closer.

"We'll find them," he whispers. "We'll save them, don't worry. And we'll make sure they'll never be able to do that to others again."

"The youngest of the cl- of Kat's siblings is only around three," Beth says, giving me an apologetic look for her slip of the tongue. "Then there's one that's between her and Little Kat. The two girls who're now in Stormborough are both 14; they're twins. I mean, technically they're all identical, but those two were created at the same time. Not counting Kat, there are only two others who're older than them."

"I think we should look for the oldest ones first. If we're lucky, they're allowed to walk outside, maybe even go on jobs like I used to do. It would make it easier to find them. I doubt they're in this town though. I would have recognised the scent."

"Yeah, I would have, too," Lennox adds. "I sometimes came across Kat's scent, but I know that well enough to be sure that it was yours. I'm not sure if it's the same for you cats, but wolves can determine the age of someone from their scent. I would have noticed if the cat shifter was younger than you."

I can't help but sigh. "I've never been out of this town. I don't have any contacts in other cities. What if all of my siblings have been sent away? How are we ever going to find them?"

"That's why you've got a team," Lily says with a reassuring smile. "I'll get in touch with my sister and some of the other succubi I met during the festival I went to. They came from all over the place, so I'm well connected now. They might only be able to tell that someone is a shifter, not what kind exactly, but having a description of you might help. If they all look like you, we should start distributing some pictures of you, and maybe of Little Kat."

"Won't that draw attention to them?" Ryker asks with a concerned frown.

I shrug. "The Pack already know me, and they know that I have freed Little Kat. They know what I look like. We do have to make sure though that any information we get is vetted. The Pack will likely try and have us walk into a trap, so any tip-offs we get could be fake. And dangerous."

"I can try and get in touch with some of my friends," Gryphon says hesitantly. "But I'm not sure how many of them are trustworthy. I'd rather keep that as a last resort."

Knowing that the others aren't aware of his species, I quickly nod, not wanting any of them to ask him questions that he'd be unable to answer. One day, he's going to tell them, but I get why he doesn't want to. His family basically run the Pack as well as similar organisations all over the country. It would be easy to suspect that he's secretly still one of them - but I know him better. I trust him.

"I might be able to use my employer's network of contacts to do some digging." Lennox runs a hand through his black hair. "I'm sure I can come up with a good excuse. And I know a couple of shifters who travel between cities. They would be able to tell me if they've ever come across a panther shifter. It's not like there's a lot of you."

I smile at him, his azure eyes reminding me of something. "Little Kat told me about a blue house that she was taken to. A blue house with a red roof."

"That shouldn't be too hard to find," Ryker says. "I doubt there are many houses like that. Although I'm not sure my cats can help with that. They see colours differently from how you do."

Interesting. As a panther, my world is a little duller than when I'm human, but I've always found colours to be pretty much the same, just less intense. I didn't know it was different for cats.

"I know a house like that." Ben has been quiet until now, but he seems happy he can finally contribute something. "It's not that far actually, near the Drowned Man pub. All the houses in that street are colourful. Rumour is to make it easier for drunks to find their home."

Bethany snickers. "I've never been to the Drowned Man, but I think it's time for a visit. How about a night out for all of us?"

CHAPTER EIGHT

It's strange to be around so many people at once. Gryphon, Lennox, Beth, Benjamin and Lily are all walking by my side, on the way to the pub. Well, not sure we're actually going to end up in there. First we need to check out that blue house.

Ryker has gone to check on his cats, taking little Pumpkin with him. I think he needs some time to process the fact that he still doesn't know whether Pumpkin will one day be able to shift. I wish we'd been able to find a definite answer. Not knowing is always worse than knowing.

It's a workday, but still, the streets are full of people on the way to their evening haunts. The area we're heading to isn't one of the nicest. Prostitutes lean against the walls, showing way too much skin, with men leering at their half-exposed boobs. Drunks are traversing the street in wiggly lines, unable to keep upright. The sun hasn't even set yet and they're already pissed.

I don't like alcohol much. It makes me lose control

of my senses, which is about the worst thing that can happen to an assassin.

Lennox hooks his arm around mine, startling me. This is a very close, very intimate gesture. Not something I do. I don't walk hand in hand with guys.

While I try and find a way to tell him gently that I don't like it, Gryphon does the same on my other side. I'm trapped between the two men. As if they've planned it.

Lily wolf-whistles from behind me. Bitch. I bet she's enjoying this. She knows how much I hate touchy-feely stuff.

If these two were any other men, I'd skewer them with my blades, but I can't. They're too valuable to hurt. I need them to save my siblings and to overthrow the Pack. That's all. The only reason. My heart beating faster at their touch has nothing to do with it.

"Once we're done, maybe we could go somewhere nice and have dinner," Gryphon mutters, just loud enough for me and Lennox to hear him.

"Are you suggesting a date?" Lennox sounds excited about that. "With both of us?"

Gryphon shrugs. "You're here, I'm here, we both want her, Kat wants us, so yes, let's do it."

I stop in my tracks, making them stumble backwards. "Wait a second. What did you just say?"

Bethany laughs as the three Meow employees walk around us. "See you at the pub."

Her and Lily snicker, and I'm tempted to throw something at them.

They leave me to my fate. Gryphon and Lennox

wait until the others are out of earshot. How nice of them.

"She's not said no," Gryphon observes. "Which means you owe me a fiver."

This time, I push them away and step back, my hands at my hips as I stare them down.

"You took bets?" I ask, incredulous at their audacity.

Lennox gives me a sheepish smile. "It kind of happened. We had a chat on how to approach the subject with you. I thought you'd immediately protest and that we'd have to try something more subtle."

"You've had a chat," I stutter, my heart and my brain fighting for dominance.

"I smelled him on you," Lennox admits. "So I cornered him. I needed to know his intentions."

"Which are good," Gryphon interjects.

"Yes, I don't think he's trying to break your heart. And neither am I. So, think you can handle both of us?"

"Not at once," Gryphon adds quickly.

Lennox smirks. "Unless you want to."

I hold up my hands, my mind whirring. Am I hallucinating this? Is this some side effect of me being in heat?

"Where does this come from, all of a sudden?"

Lennox's smile falls a little. "I thought I'd shown you that I want you. Not just my wolf. Me too. And I understand that it's overwhelming and if you need more time, that's okay. I just wanted to stake my claim before the other two make you theirs."

Instinctively, I draw my two blades, pointing them at their throats. "I'm nobody's. Neither of you is going to claim me. I'm my own woman and you better understand that."

Gryphon blinks at me, his beautiful green eyes full of emotion that I can't quite pinpoint. "You can do the claiming if you want," he says hoarsely. "You're in charge."

Lennox stares at me for a moment, then inclines his head. "You're in charge."

I don't know what to say. Or do. Old Kat would have run. Probably after poisoning them, making them suffer for a couple of hours.

Kat-in-Heat, though, wants them. Not poisoned, but alive and virile. With me.

I look at the two of them. Gryphon, dressed in black as always, with his scarred face and grassy green eyes. Lennox, broader and taller than the other man, with hair as black as Gryphon's clothes and azure blue eyes that seem to sparkle when he looks at me. The two of them are gorgeous, and the thought of having both of them as mine makes me tremble. But there's also a tiny voice in my head, a greedy voice, reminding me that there's someone else. Ryker. If I take their offer and go on a date with the two of them, wouldn't that be unfair to the cat shifter? I want to be with him too. Yes, I'm greedy as fuck, but my current hormonal state is entirely unapologetic about that.

I take a deep breath. "I'm not going on a date with you today."

I watch them closely as disappointment mirrors on both of their faces. Yes, they really mean it. Really want me. That's reassuring.

"Because Ryker isn't here. Talk to him, add him to your weird man-talk thing, and then ask me out again."

Lennox laughs in relief. "I was wondering about him, but I didn't want to progress to three of us until you'd accepted us two."

Gryphon isn't looking quite as happy about it as the wolf.

"Gryphon?" I ask softly. "Are you okay with that?"

He nods. "Yes, just hadn't realised... Yes, I'm okay with it. We'll talk to him. We-"

A scream cuts through his words.

I exchange a look with the guys, then we run towards the screams, towards the pub where the others are.

❀ ❀ ❀ ❀ ❀ ❀

LILY IS ON THE GROUND, HOLDING HER ARM. HER DRESS is covered in blood, but it doesn't seem to be hers. Bethany is standing in front of her, wielding a knife, snarling at anyone trying to get close. Benjamin is nowhere to be seen.

"What happened?" I shout as soon as I'm in earshot.

"A guy attacked her. Ben's ran after him." Beth points to a narrow alley to her right.

"Lily, are you alright?"

She nods, but the grimace on her face tells of the pain she must be in. "Go, don't worry about me."

As much as I would like to make sure she's safe, I know she's right. I hand Lily one of my knives, just in case the attacker returns.

"Bethany, stay with her. Gryphon, Lennox, you're with me."

I run into the dark alley, extending my cat senses, following Benjamin's scent. The street is getting narrower the further we run. There are old houses here, some more shacks than actual stone houses, and I doubt many of them are still inhabited. The perfect place to hide.

Benjamin has left a potent trail that's easy to follow. His scent is getting sweatier; I think even humans might be able to smell him by now.

We turn a corner and there he is, panting, looking up at the smooth wall of a house.

"He climbed up there," he calls out breathlessly. "I couldn't follow."

"Go back to the others," I shout, but I don't stop running. I launch myself into the air and start to climb. I find footholds where most people would slip and fall. Gryphon overtakes me, climbing up as fast and light-footed as a spider. Call me impressed. Lennox stays on the ground, following the same strategy we used to employ back in the Pack. I'd follow on the rooftops, he'd be in the streets, cutting off our target's escape route.

There's a faint scent on the stone wall, giving me an idea of what to expect our mark to look like. He's human, male, must be past his prime. Not as much testosterone as younger men.

I reach the edge of the roof and pull myself up until I'm crouching on the uneven tiles. There's moss growing between them; nobody has been up here in a while. It makes spotting the man's footprints easy, although I wouldn't need them since his scent is getting stronger. His feet are massive, leading me to think that he must be half a giant. Or maybe he's tiny with oversized feet, who knows.

Gryphon is already jumping from this roof to another, landing in an elegant roll that makes me almost jealous. The way he gracefully jumps to his feet and continues running without pause is nothing but beautiful. Far in the distance, at least twenty houses away from me, is a dark figure. That must be our prey.

My fingers itch, my claws threatening to come out. My prey. I'm hunting with my mates. I love that thought.

A meow breaks from my lips and I increase my pace, flying from roof to roof, my feet steady whenever they touch a roof despite the slippery tiles. I've done this all my life.

By the time I catch up with Gryphon, the man is only five or so roofs in front of us. Easy.

Lennox is running down below, but he's a couple of houses away; the alleyways must not allow him to follow us in a straight line. No matter, we're faster than our prey and Gryphon and I will be enough to take him down. No matter his big feet.

"This is fun," Gryphon shouts, barely out of breath.

I shoot him a grin. He's right, this is exhilarating. Of course, it's also terrible that Lily got hurt, but running over the roofs with Gryphon by my side is simply amazing. I kind of don't want it to stop.

"Stop!" I shout when we're only one roof behind our target. He half turns, misses a step, and as if in slow motion he stumbles, falls, glides down the tiles, hangs above the drain pipe for a moment, then it gives way and he falls.

"Shit," Gryphon mutters and jumps over to the roof. I follow him, peeking down the wall. The man is lying on the ground, his legs bent in wholly unnatural angles. He's alive though; I can smell his fear and pain.

I could take the time and climb down the wall, but who knows how long this guy will still be alive. I need answers.

I pull on my cat strength and jump. Cats always land on all fours. We don't get injured from falling. We're cats, after all, the perfect jumping and climbing machines.

Brushing off the dirt from my hands, I stalk towards the man. He groans in pain. The predator in me loves that sound. I want to make him whimper, beg for relief. He hurt my friend. He's going to suffer.

I crouch down by his head. He looks me straight in the eyes. His are bloodshot and there's a trickle of blood coming from one of his nostrils. Maybe he's got a head injury. I need to be fast.

"Why did you hurt the girl?" I growl.

His eyes widen, but then his mouth curves into an ugly smile.

"She was pretty," he rasps.

I sense Gryphon and Lennox behind me, but they give us space, letting me deal with this bastard. Since he seems to need some help telling me what happened, I pull one of my knives and press it against his throat. His smile fades. Good.

"Why?" I repeat.

"I told ya. She's pretty. I like breakin' pretty things."

I stare at him. Is he for real?

"She was with two other people. I doubt you just attacked her because she was pretty."

He coughs and a few droplets of blood are catapulted into the air. He doesn't have long. I can smell the blood inside of him. He's got internal injuries, and in combination with the head wound, I doubt I'm going to be doing the killing. Nature will take its course.

"She smiled at me," he groans. "She invited me ta hurt her."

"What the fuck?"

"She wanted it. She loved it."

Okay, he's batshit crazy. Deluded. The world will be better off without him. Breaking Lily's arm because she smiled at him.

"He's lying," Gryphon says from behind me. He steps to my side and his musky scent fills my senses. No, not now. Concentrate, Kat. Not on his alluring scent, but on the dying man in front of you.

"May I?"

I nod. Maybe Gryphon's siren talents will make the man talk.

Gryphon kneels by the man's side and puts a hand on his bloody forehead. "Tell me the truth," he says sharply. His eyes grow dark as if clouds are passing over a grassy meadow. Storm clouds that will bring destruction and pain.

The man on the ground shudders. He seems to be

fighting Gryphon, but then his eyes turn glassy and his expression blank.

"Was told ta split ya up. The others will have looked after yer friends by now. The order was ta kidnap them, or kill them if they make too much trouble. Pity I never got ta have fun with the lass. She's pretty."

His eyelids flutter and I know he's dead before I focus on his missing heartbeat.

Fuck.

I jump up and put my knife back in its sheath. "We need to find the others."

This time, I don't hold back my cat. I shift in one fluid motion, amazed at how easy it feels this way. Maybe it's the worry for my friends.

I run, hoping that I'm not too late.

CHAPTER NINE

They aren't where we left them. Lennox is by my side, sniffing the ground, his wolf senses at high alert. Gryphon isn't here yet; we're faster than him when shifted.

I scan the area. There aren't any people. It was a busy street when we left, but now it lies abandoned. Something bad has happened. I can smell it.

I focus on Lily's scent, the one I know best. It's strongest in the spot where she was sitting earlier, cradling her arm. I shouldn't have left her. Benjamin's scent is all over the place; he must have returned to the girls while we were chasing the bad guy. Did they take all three of them? Or did they split them up? Are they still alive?

I shut those thoughts away and focus on my hunter instincts. I imagine them as my prey, and immediately, my vision changes. Scents turn into colourful lines and shapes around me, with the ones I recognise as bright, glowing ropes. They're intertwined and I breathe a sigh of relief. They were together when they were taken. Other lines surround them, stronger than those of simple passerby. Those must be the assailants. Six of them. Two for each of my Meow employees. All three of them know how to handle themselves, but they're not hand-to-hand combat people. Benjamin works best in the shadows, thieving and occasionally doing a bit of killing. Lily seduces and elicits truths that people don't want to part with. Bethany poisons and loves a bit of torture. But facing off armed attackers, being outnumbered? I'm not sure how they fared. Lily had my knife and Bethany her own, and I'm sure Benjamin carried some kind of weapon. We're Meow, after all, none of us ever walk around unarmed. Beth always has some poison darts tucked away. She's good with them, almost as good as me. Maybe they let themselves be taken to find out what they want from them. Positive thinking, that's it.

Lennox whines and scratches at the ground. I wish I could communicate with him when he's a wolf. But as it is, sign language and miming will have to do. I head over to where he's pointing with his paws. A drop of blood. I sniff it. Not my friends. Good. That means they managed to injure one of their attackers, although it can't have been a deep wound, with only this one tiny drop of blood. Still, it helps with getting an even better trace on him. I breathe in deep, committing the scent to mind. One of the lines surrounding us turns thicker. That's the one I'm going to follow.

Lennox barks and starts walking in the direction of

the very scent I'm focusing on. Oh well. I'll let him take that one. I'm a gentle(wo)man after all. Sometimes.

I walk along the street for a few yards, watching how the scents change. They split in two directions when I get to a crossing. Bethany and Lily have been taken down an alleyway to my right while Benjamin continued straight ahead. There are three of the attackers with either group. Why did three of them stay with Benjamin? He's a scrawny boy, hardly a threat.

The silence is bothering me. No people at all. In one way, it's good because nobody will be shocked by seeing a panther and a wolf running down the street. But where is everyone? How did they manage to get rid of all the drunks and revellers? The Drowned Man pub is just around the corner, so there must be people wanting to get there.

I hear Gryphon's panting before he arrives. He's fast, but not as fast as us shifters, despite his other skills. He skids to a stop and looks around, taking in the scene.

"Where are the people?" he asks, voicing my thoughts.

I try to shrug, but I'm not sure if he can interpret a panther's shrug. My shoulders aren't where they are when I'm human. It's a pity Ryker isn't here to translate.

"Do you have their scent?"

I nod and point ahead and to the alley with one paw.

"I think we should stick together," he says, looking down the dark alley. It's pretty much identical to the one we followed to race after Lily's attacker.

I nod again and meow at Lennox. He pads over, his

nose close to the ground. I've always wondered if he visualises scents like I do or if it's different for him.

"Which one shall we follow?" Gryphon asks.

I sniff. The stronger scent, the one from the injured man, heads to the right. I wave my paw and start walking. I don't run, preferring to save my strength and keep my full focus on tracking.

The others shadow me, easily falling into a formation. Gryphon keeps watch, making sure nobody surprises us. Lennox also sniffs for scents, my backup in case I lose the trace.

We must make a strange sight. A human-looking siren, a werewolf and a panther walking along a street at night, hunting bad guys. Sounds like a fairy tale. Or a superhero film. Except that we're no heroes. Not in the slightest. Heroes don't kill for fun. They don't run assassin agencies. And they certainly don't lust after three men at once.

The longer we walk, the stronger the scent becomes. It can't have been too long that they passed by here. Around corners we go, through narrow alleys and archways that look like they're about to crumble. This is becoming more slum than town. I've been here before, obviously, but since most of my marks live in posher parts of town, it's been a while since I last had deadlines in this area. Mostly to get supplies for poisons or to meet people interested in employing me. They always assume that I favour a place like this to meet up, while actually, I'd much rather have our encounters in their homes or offices. It gives me an impression of who they are and how much I can charge.

"Wait, I know this street," Gryphon mutters. "A guy I once did a job for lives here. Actually, maybe he just meets people here, I can't imagine him living in a dirt hole like this."

Since I can't reply or ask questions, I give him an encouraging meow.

"He runs a network of thieves and lowlives. Humans only. He calls himself the Spider and his people are the Web. He thought I was human, obviously, otherwise, he'd never have worked with me. He believes there are too many shifters in this business and that humans should be the ones ruling the criminal underworld." He snickers. "As if they'd be strong enough. I glamoured him into paying me three times the promised rate and he didn't even realise."

I wonder if he's the one who's kidnapped my friends. Maybe he feels threatened by Meow, a supernatural assassin agency? That seems a little stupid, though. And too sophisticated. Splitting us up, knowing that we'd be here – someone had to have been following us from our headquarters and that means they are good, really good. None of us noticed, after all, although I have to admit that I was a little distracted by the guys. The Kat-in-Heat thing is making me incompetent at my job. I've always noticed when I've had a tail. A metaphorical one. I always know when I have an actual physical tail. I snort at my silliness in frustration. I need to concentrate.

I continue on, following the ever stronger growing scent trail. It disappears through a low door in a building that looks like it's about to collapse. A few bricks are already scattered all around its walls, along with shattered roof tiles. The next storm will be the end of this house.

Lennox sniffs the air, growling softly. He must be smelling the same that I do. A lot of males close by, full of testosterone. Not just the three whose scents we've followed here. Many more; at least five others. I hope they haven't harmed Lily and Bethany.

We need to be fast. This might be a trap – no, this most certainly *is* a trap – but I don't have a choice. My friends are in danger. We need to get them out and then go after Benjamin. I hope he'll understand that we went for the two women first. Not because they're weaker, but because the scent of their attacker was stronger and because it makes sense to rescue two allies first, who can then help us.

I want to stay a panther, but I'm too big to sneak around these small, unsteady buildings. I might do more harm than good.

Taking a deep breath, I steel myself for the pain and begin the shift. It doesn't hurt at all. What the fuck is happening? It's never been painless, never felt as easy as this. Never. Is it my heat hormones? Or did my near-death change something? This is the first time I've shifted since then. I was scared before, especially after meowing as a human. Ending up as some kind of permanent hybrid didn't sound like a good idea at the time.

Lennox shoots me a questioning glance. His blue eyes are glinting in the dark.

"You stay shifted for now," I whisper. "Gryphon and

I will stake out the place and go in first, then you can follow and do some slashing and biting."

Lennox bares his fangs in agreement.

I pull my knives, glad for the strange shifter magic that lets me keep my clothes and weapons, and walk to the small door. I lean against it, listening for sounds from the other side. Nothing.

"I'll check it out from above," Gryphon mutters quietly and deftly climbs up the wall of the house opposite. I watch his lithe figure as he makes his way to the roof, looking as if it's as easy as a walk in the park. Once he's at the top, he looks around, searching the area.

Lennox sniffs around the house, his ears twitching as he listens for anything that might help us.

Gryphon points to something beyond the house we're watching. His lips move and I focus on my cat senses to hear him. "Their actual hideout is behind. You need to go through the old building and then you'll get to the one where they're waiting."

I chuckle. No way am I simply going to walk through that door. I bet there are traps on the other side. No, I'm going to take the upper route as well. The roof of the dilapidated house looks too unsafe to walk on, so I climb the wall of the neighbouring building, which is two storeys higher and hopefully more stable.

Lennox gives me a little whine when I look down on him.

"Go and see if you can find some cats in the vicinity," I whisper, knowing that he'll be able to hear me despite the distance. "It would be good to have Ryker here as backup."

He nods, waggles his tail and runs off. I could have searched for cats myself but I'm already on the roof and I don't want Lennox to shift back yet. Having a wolf fight by my side might come in handy.

I hate not knowing what awaits us. Usually, I'd stake out this house, taking hours to watch who comes and goes, figuring out escape routes and weak spots. Now, we have to act fast and there's no time to play it safe.

All my cat senses are telling me is that Bethany and Lily are in the tall house behind the crumbling smaller one, which can only be accessed through that door or from above. As I slowly make my way along the roof, a small, dirty courtyard comes into view. It's empty except for some white plastic sacks in one corner. I wonder what's inside those. It would be disappointing if it were only rubbish. I'd be much more interested in body parts.

Gryphon has jumped over to my side of the street and now joins me, crouching low next to me. His scent fills my nose and I breathe in deep. Not distracting at all.

"Can you tell how many there are?" he whispers.

I shake my head. "I'm not quite close enough to smell them and they're being very quiet." *And your scent is distracting me.* But I don't say that. He doesn't need to know what kind of effect he has on me. I think the Kat-in-Heat is getting worse. I'm on a rooftop, two of my friends have been kidnapped, and I'm thinking of Gryphon's alluring scent and how I would like to jump him here and now. It can't continue like that or I'll be out of business soon.

"But Lily and Bethany are in there?"

"Yes, their trail went through the door and the little house. It was so strong that I think they must be close, probably in that building or at least not far from here." I turn to him, although looking at his scarred, beautiful face only makes my urges stronger. "How many people can you influence at once?"

"Unless I start singing, two at the max, depending on how strong-minded they are. Sirens can control more than just two people if they know them and have used their powers on them continuously. It makes them more perceptible. My father had around twenty men who he was able to steer and even fully control if necessary. I'm a little out of practice, though."

"What happens if you sing?"

I think back to his song at his place, how his music quite literally touched my body... I doubt he's going to give the kidnappers an orgasm. Although that might distract them enough for us to get the two women.

"I can't push a specific command through my song, just an emotion, a feeling. And I can't control who reacts to it, which means all of you would be affected. You probably least of them all, and I'm not sure about Lily, but Bethany is human and would succumb to my song, making a rescue much harder. If we can avoid it, I'd rather not sing and have it as a last resort."

I nod. "Can you do any emotion?"

"It works best if it fits the situation. In this case, I'd

use fear, while in other cases, something positive works better."

Something seems to get lodged in my throat. *Something positive.* Like making me completely and entirely aroused. Making me lose my mind. I hope he's going to give me another show of his talents when we're alone. Not here on a roof.

He clears his throat, and from the heat in his gaze, I sense that he was thinking of the same thing. "What now?"

The predator in me rises to the surface as I stare down at the house where my friends are being held. "Now, we kill."

CHAPTER TEN

Gryphon drops down into the courtyard, landing in a graceful crouch. He's got his scimitar in one hand and a short dagger in the other. He's the only person I know who fights with that curved sword, but he says he's found it to be the most effective for his style of fighting. Each to their own. I wrap my hands around the hilts of my own daggers. I can almost feel them lusting for blood.

He looks up at me and I give him a short nod. It's time to begin our assault. I take a few steps back and let my panther's strength seep into my muscles. Then I run to the edge of the roof. And jump.

I fly over the courtyard, but it's almost too far, even with the added strength. I stretch in mid-flight, letting my claws shoot out, and then I'm clinging to the edge of the roof, my legs dangling, my claws half-embedded in some tiles. That was close. With a groan, I pull myself up onto the roof. I think I broke a claw. Oh well. I let them shift back into fingernails, and while there's a drop of blood on one of them, everything seems to be fine.

The door to the courtyard opens with a creak and two men pour outside. Grunts would be a fitting description. As wide and bullish as oxen, and probably just as stupid.

Gryphon cuts one of them down before they can even react, but the second manages to yell for help before the scimitar relieves his head from his body. Now that I'm on top of the roof, I can sense the people inside. Eight men, two women, not counting the two bodies on the ground. Totally doable.

The two female and one male scents are further away and slightly muffled. A basement, probably. Good, that means they won't be able to take the women out of the house too quickly. Unless they have tunnels in their basement. I think back to the Kindler case. How I hate underground tunnels.

While Gryphon waits for reinforcements, acting as the distraction just like we agreed, I run to the other side of the roof, where a dust-covered attic window is waiting for me. I don't bother being quiet and careful with opening it. I flip my dagger in my hand and crash the hilt against the glass. It shatters; shards of glass raining down into the attic.

My senses tell me that nobody's in the dark room, so I drop down, avoiding most of the shards. My leather boots have thick soles because of exactly these kind of situations. It happens more often than you'd think.

A narrow, steep staircase leads down to the first floor. Maybe I should get one of those for my own attic, but then, I like my trap door. It stops people from harassing me too frequently.

The sounds of fighting make me quicken my pace. Gryphon should be fine, but let's not dawdle. Hopefully, Lennox will join him soon. The first floor is just as empty as the attic. Everyone's either trying to get into the courtyard or down in the basement.

I sneak down the stairs. At the end of a short corridor leading to what smells like a dirty kitchen stands a man, his back to me. Nice. Prey that likes to make it easy for me. I debate whether to use one of my poison darts for a moment, but no, I'm in the mood for some blood. My panther is yearning for a fight.

My dagger almost jumps into my hand and I throw it in one smooth motion. It embeds itself in the man's neck, snapping his spinal cord. He collapses to the ground with a dull thud, unable to even scream in pain. I run over, pull my knife from his prone body and, feeling nice, cut his throat rather than have him suffocate to death. I know, I'm far too kind.

Relying on my sense of smell, I follow Lily's scent back along the corridor until I reach a bookcase. Really? How predictable. I pull on the book that has the most potent scent and the bookshelf detaches from the wall, revealing a hidden door. As I said, pathetic.

On the other side of the door, a staircase leads into a dark, damp smelling basement. The women's scent is strong now. There's only one guard. Did they expect we'd just let them take my friends without a fight?

He stinks of testosterone, sweat and something else, something that seems familiar but foreign at the same time. I turn around two corners until his scent becomes so strong I know that he's close. I don't make a sound as I ready my knives. This time, I might play with him for a while. The other death was too fast, not satisfying enough. Blood helps make a death experience feel more fulfilling.

That's what I should add to my business cards. *Katriona Feln, the best provider of death experiences. Discover the only true way to die. A five-star experience that will leave you breathless.*

I'm procrastinating. Why is it so hard to focus today? First, I was too obsessed with wanting to hump Gryphon, and now I'm thinking about how to market my business. Focus, Kat. Your friends are in danger. This isn't the time to lose track of what's important.

I steel my mind and step around the corner, bringing me face to face with a beast of a man. He's massive, his shoulders twice as broad as my own, his legs like tree trunks, his face hidden by a wild beard. Tattoos snake up and down his bare arms, most of them crude and badly done. His eyes don't gleam with any intelligence. He's their guard dog, the muscle, not someone who actually controlled this operation. Good, that means I can kill him without regrets. I wouldn't want to miss the chance to interrogate whoever is in charge here.

He doesn't look surprised and picks up at an axe leaning against the wall. It's almost as tall as I am. My knives aren't going to be much use against it, so let's be quick. Before he can properly lift the axe, I jump forward, my knives extended, ready to pierce his large stomach.

For such a big man, he moves surprisingly fast. He blocks my attack with one arm while he swings the axe with the other. My knives slide over his leather armguard, leaving deep gashes but barely reaching his skin. Out of balance, I stumble forward, but catch myself just in time to evade the axe by crouching low. The metal swooshes over my head and a solitary hair slowly falls to the floor. That was close; I hadn't expected him to be able to swing the axe with just one arm. This guy is strong.

Since I'm already on the ground, I go for the closest target: his legs. He's not wearing any armour there, just simple trousers big enough to be used as flour bags. My knives slice across the back of his knees and down he goes, falling forward.

Fuck. I'd expected him to topple in the other direction, but the weight of the axe must have messed with physics.

I roll to my right, just about evading his massive body. He grunts as he hits the ground, but he keeps hold of his axe. He's not done yet. I jump to my feet, finally feeling like I've got an advantage now that he's no longer towering over me. I could jab him with some poison darts to make it quick, but this is far too much fun. Adrenaline is coursing through my veins, making me feel more alive than I have ever since I woke up from my near-death experience. This is why I do this job. The danger, the excitement. And finally, a challenge. Most marks aren't prepared for me or have no physical strength, but this man, he's actually a match for me.

I grin as I watch him shuffle and turn until he's

kneeling, now almost as tall as me. His eyes burn with hatred and pain. The smell of blood fills my nostrils and I can't help but smile. He's still bleeding, losing strength with every drop of ruby-red liquid dripping onto the floor. I need to hurry up, or he won't be a challenge for much longer. I want to enjoy this.

"You'll pay for that," he grunts.

I quirk an eyebrow. "Make me."

He lifts the axe with one hand as easily as he did when he was still standing. The sharp blade glints in the dim light. It's not tasted blood yet. Maybe I should let it nip me, just for fun. Pain makes me even more feral.

The man tries to swing his axe, but he's too close to the ground and doesn't get the angle right. The blade crashes into the wall, making splinters of stone fall onto the floor.

"Want one of my knives?"

He glares at me. And then his eyes turn yellow. Fucking yellow. How the heck? He's human. He smells human. Is this some kind of mutation? A freak of nature? Or is he a species I haven't encountered before, one that can masquerade as human?

"What are you?" I snarl, gripping my knives a little harder. The unknown excites me, but I'm angry that I didn't realise before.

He smiles, exposing sharp teeth. I swear they were smooth before. His canines didn't protrude like they do now, pointed and dangerous looking.

"Something new," he hisses and then he's on his feet as if I never injured his legs. What the fuck? He's healed; the smell of blood is almost gone. I've never seen anything like it. Shifters can heal, yes, but it takes time, it's not instantaneous as this. One thing is for certain, he's not human. Not in the slightest.

"Tell me," I challenge him, waiting for his attack. I won't charge him until I know who or what he is. I need this information more than I need to see him suffer.

His grin widens. "I'm your death."

He attacks, swinging his axe like it's light as a stick of wood. I barely manage to evade his strike by crouching low. He laughs and raises his axe once more, ready to strike. I decide it's enough. Pulling a dart from my collar, I jab it in his leg. It's not a deadly one; I need him alive for now. It's going to paralyse him in three, two, one…

Nothing happens. He didn't even notice me pricking him, but now his axe is racing towards me, ready to split me in two. I jump, sliding through his wide-open legs, rolling until I can flip to my legs. I'm kind of proud of that move, but not for long. He turns faster than his bulk should allow and continues his attack.

I don't have a chance to take the offensive; I'm busy making sure that he doesn't cleave me into a limbless, headless Kat. I still enjoy our dance, but it's getting frustrating. Usually, I'm the one in charge, but this is the very opposite. He's stronger and it hurts to realise that.

This time, I take two darts and flick them at his throat. He manages to pull one out before much of the poison can reach his bloodstream, but misses the other. I wait with bated breath, hoping that this time, there will be some kind of effect. My darts should work on shifters, not as effective as on humans, but still well enough to slow them down and put them out of commission for a while. Long enough for me to get the upper hand.

Not with him, though. He laughs as if my actions amuse him.

"Got anything better?" he growls and stalks towards me. His canines are even longer now, reaching all the way over his bottom lip. He's changing while we're fighting, and who knows what the end result will be. I need to act fast.

My knives gripped tight, I launch myself forward, evading his strike and diving under his arm, stabbing one blade into the soft spot in his armpit and the other along his chest, just above where his armour ends. That one won't hurt him much, but I want to see how fast he heals. And the armpit one is the one I put all my strength into anyway. It's a great place to make someone bleed. A lot. And yes, blood sprays all over my face even as I retreat.

He yelps, a pitiful sound, reminding me of a wounded dog. He stares at his arm, hanging limply along his body. I must have severed some sinew and nerves. Good. That should stop him for a while.

I don't wait to see the effect, just in case he heals too fast. Knowing that my paralysing darts are ineffective on him, I take the deadly ones this time. Two, for good measure. If he dies, Beth can dissect him and we might still manage to learn more about what he is. I'm becoming more and more aware that Lily and Bethany are held down here in the basement, and that Gryphon hasn't joined me yet, meaning he's still busy fighting the other men upstairs. Or injured. But no, I would have heard it if he'd called for help. Where the hell is Lennox? He should be back by now. How hard is it to find a cat?

The darts embed themselves in his upper arm, the uninjured one. He doesn't seem to realise, still staring at his other one. The blood flow is already getting less; he's healing. Damn. I've never seen anyone heal this fast. It shouldn't be possible.

Three, two, one… he stumbles. His knees buckle and he's back on the ground, but he's still very much alive. I shot him with two deadly darts and he looks as if he's barely affected. I'm running out of darts. Not good, but it can't be helped. Hopefully, I won't need any after I'm done with this guy. Let's hope there aren't more of him.

I shoot my last two deadly darts at him, then jump and land on him, toppling him to his back. My knives bite into his shoulders, close enough to his neck to sever all the important stuff.

He stares up at me, his yellow eyes filled with hate, and then his life bleeds out of him. He stills and I hear his heart beat a final time.

Dead. Finally.

I step off his prone body and sheathe my knives, turning away from him. Time to free my friends.

That's when his heart starts beating again.

CHAPTER ELEVEN

I throw his head as far away from his body as possible. That should keep him dead. I hope. Maybe his body will rise and randomly start slashing around with the axe he's still clutching in his lifeless hand. I pry it from his thick fingers and take it with me towards the room at the end of the dark corridor.

Lily and Beth are behind the thick iron door; I can smell them.

"Girls?" I shout. "You alright?"

"We're fine!"

Lily's voice is muffled, but she sounds healthy enough.

Annoyingly, the big guy didn't carry any keys on him, but I have my trusted lockpicks. Just when the door springs open, footsteps behind me announce someone approaching. I sniff the air. Gryphon and Lennox. Finally.

"What took you so-"

I swallow my words. They're covered in blood. Lots

and lots of blood. It cakes their hair, soaks their clothes, leaves a trail in their path. That's going to be one long shower.

"One of them was a little bit of work," Lennox says with a wry smile. He points at the head on the floor and gives it a little kick. "I see you had one of them as well."

Gryphon inspects the headless body. "Nice work. I assume your poisons didn't work either?"

I shake my head. "Not in the slightest. Beheading seemed to do it, though."

He chuckles. "Yeah, same for ours. Except that it took me three of his resurrections to figure that out."

"Feel like letting us out anytime soon?" Beth shouts from behind me. "It's getting cold in here."

Cold? It's rather warm down here. But I see why she said that when I enter their cell. They're naked, both of them. They didn't even get to keep their underwear.

"Guys, keep back," I tell the guys before they can follow me. I know Lily wouldn't have a problem with men seeing her naked, but I'm not sure about Bethany. And to be honest, I don't want the men to see anyone except for me that way. No more naked girls for them. I'm a cat, I'm possessive by nature.

I pick the handcuffs keeping Lily and Beth shackled to the wall, before sending the men to find some clothes in the house.

While we wait for them to return, I sit down on the wooden bench and rub the blood off my knives. They'll get a proper polish when we're back home, and they probably need some sharpening as well after being stopped by that leather armguard. I love looking after my weapons. It's a calming procedure that lets me clear my head and focus on a simple task that doesn't require much thinking.

"What happened to Ben?" Beth asks after a moment of silence. "They split us up as soon as they'd subdued us."

"We're going after him once we're done turning this house upside down. They were fools to lead us here. It seems to have been used as a hideout and I want to gather as much intelligence as I can before we leave."

"Why did they take our clothes?" Lily asks. "They didn't try to hurt us, just made us strip and then chained us to the wall."

"One of them was strange. He had some shifter characteristics but wasn't a shifter, not a real one anyway. I wonder if his kind can do the same kind of tracking as proper shifters can. Taking your clothes would provide them with an easy way to track you no matter where you are. You wore them while you were attacked, which means you likely sweated and left a strong smell on them."

"Are you saying some weird creature is going to sniff my clothes?" Bethany asks incredulously.

I shrug. "I've done that before when trying to find people. Actually, I'm going to see if I can find some clothes here that don't belong to one of the men we killed. Might be helpful later."

Not that I'm looking forward to sniffing bad people's underwear, but sometimes life throws you a murderer's dirty y-fronts and you just have to deal with it.

"If they now have access to our scents, does that

mean they'll keep coming for us?" Lily cradles her broken arm. We need to get her to a doctor. Succubi don't have any better healing powers than humans do, so she must be in a lot of discomfort.

"We'll figure out what they want," I promise her. "And I'll make sure that they won't hurt you again. They'll be too dead to get close to any of us."

"That's reassuring. Unless they turn into zombies." Beth snickers. I'd hate to tell her that the man outside was kind of a zombie. If you define that as coming back from the dead. Luckily, the decapitation seems to have done the trick.

Lily rolls her shoulders, her expression pained. "Why does this always happen when we want to have a night out? We keep ending up in trouble."

I snort. "You call this trouble? I've had much worse."

"I can confirm that's correct," Lennox says from behind me with a chuckle. "She's done much, much worse."

I step out of the room to see him and frown. "How would you even know? It's not like you've been around much the last ten years."

Oops, that sounded a little bitter.

He raises an eyebrow, probably trying to figure out if I'm angry with him for some reason or not. I give him a tight smile and that pretty eyebrow lowers itself to a normal level.

"I know my Kat," he replies softly. "I can't imagine your life getting any less dangerous after I left, on the contrary. Am I wrong?"

"Nah," I mutter, hating to prove him right. "But

that's not important right now. We need to search this place and then find Benjamin."

Lennox hands me a stack of clothes. "That's the best I could find. And the other two are already turning the house upside down."

"Two?"

"Ryker's arrived. It took his cats forever to bring him here. He joined us just when we'd finished dispatching that creature."

"Which is why my clothes aren't bloody!" Ryker shouts from above. Wow, his hearing is excellent. "Kat, if you want to hug someone, take me!"

"Why would I want to hug someone?" I ask in genuine confusion, before remembering my little heat problem. Right now, I don't feel horny. Wow. That's the first time in forever that I don't want to jump Lennox and take him right against the wall. It must be all the excitement and adrenaline. I shall have to remember that. Killing someone lessens your libido. Who'd have thought.

I can't help but smile at that development. It's an easy cure. Killing is free, fun and less effort than screwing someone. Although I have to admit, it's not quite as much fun as I could have with my guys.

LENNOX, BETHANY AND LILY STAY BEHIND TO SEARCH the house. Then Lily is going to be accompanied to the hospital.

She's not someone who likes to make a fuss, but I've

instructed Bethany to use any threats she can come up with to make sure that Lily lets herself be examined and treated. Since Lennox has shifted once tonight already, it's better if he stays human for now, which is why he's the one staying with the girls. I doubt anyone is going to try and attack them again, not today, anyway, but if they do, he should be able to handle it, even without shifting to his wolf. And of course, Ryker's cats will be following them.

The rest of us have returned to the street where our friends got abducted. The revellers have returned, making it harder to pick up Benjamin's scent among the smell of alcohol, sweat and piss. If I didn't share a house with the thief, it might have been almost impossible to follow his trail, but I smell him every day and know exactly what I'm looking for.

Some of the people around us give us some strange glances, but we didn't have time for Gryphon to get cleaned up properly. He's donned a new shirt and jeans, but there's blood in his hair and on his boots (he didn't want to part with those). Still, this isn't an area of town where blood is something rare. Even now, I can hear several ongoing fights and smell at least two bleeding victims somewhere close by.

It takes us ten minutes to follow the trail through small alleyways and across a busy road until we get to the warehouse district. There's not much here besides, well, warehouses, as well as some smaller factories. Ryker's chocolate factory is pretty close from where we are now and I kind of wish we had time to stop by and play with the kittens.

Two cats are walking by Ryker's side, but I don't know either of them. He's attracted a wider following recently and a lot of newbies have joined his family. I'm going to have to ask him to introduce me later on. I want to know my co-workers' names.

The scent leads us to the newest looking warehouse in the vicinity. It's a shiny metal building with a glass roof. How impractical. Or is it some kind of greenhouse?

But no, the metal walls would make it a boiling heat trap.

"Ever seen this place before?" I ask the men.

"I've walked past it but never taken a closer look," Ryker says with a tone of regret. "I've checked out most of the other buildings here to scavenge, but this one has better security than all of the others combined."

We keep to the shadows and I'm glad it's night. There are a couple of spotlights illuminating the ground around the warehouse, but one of them is faulty, giving us a dark space to hide and make plans.

"Can you feel that?" Gryphon suddenly asks.

"Feel what?"

My senses aren't picking up anything out of the ordinary.

"You don't have an urge to turn and walk away from here?"

I shake my head. "Should I?"

He grimaces. "Yes, if you were human, you would. It's a siren technology. Low wave recordings of a siren's song, making anyone getting too close suddenly decide that they have somewhere better to be. I shouldn't be surprised that it's not working on the two of you."

"A recording?" Ryker asks. "Shouldn't we be able to hear that?"

"It's barely loud enough to even pick up on sensors," Gryphon explains. "If you got close to the speakers up near the roof, you might be able to sense it, but not down here."

"Fascinating," I mutter. "Could we install something similar at Meow? Not turning people away, but making them pay more for my services?"

The guys stare at me. Then Gryphon starts to laugh, genuine happiness shining in his eyes. "You're something special, Kat."

I shrug. "Just trying to make a living."

Without warning, Ryker wraps an arm around me and pulls me close. I could fight him, of course, but it feels too good to resist. His lips are on mine in an instant and I soak in his taste. Fresh milk and catnip with a hint of cinnamon.

"Stop it," Gryphon suddenly growls. I don't think it's because this is an inappropriate time or place, but because he's feeling left out. "No kissing until we have our date and talk about this."

With a last nudge of my tongue against Ryker's, I step back, frowning at Gryphon. "This?"

He waves his arm at the two of us. "This. You, him, me, Lennox. This."

I sigh. "Do we really have to talk about it? Can't we just, you know, accept you're all mine and move on?"

The guys look at each other.

"No," Gryphon grunts. "We're going to talk this through at our date. Preferably tomorrow. Or tonight. As soon as possible."

Ryker shrugs. "I've lived as a cat, and our females take as many males as they want, but now that I've shifted, I don't feel the same nonchalance about it all. I think having a chat with all of us present would be good."

I sigh. Men. They always need to make everything so complicated.

"Alright then, a date. But there needs to be good food. And wine."

Gryphon nods. "Deal. I know just the place. 8pm?"

"How about noon?" Ryker suggests. "The sooner, the better. I don't know how much I can last with smelling her in heat like that. Unless we remove the no kissing rule, then 8pm is fine."

"I'm not in heat," I protest, but him mentioning it has reminded my hormones that I am, in fact, in heat. Fuck. I'd hoped the killing's anti-libido effect would persist for a little longer. My insides clench at realising how close the two men are standing to me. How easy it would be to pull them both close, sandwiched in their midst, and do all sorts of fun and naughty things with them.

A scream pierces the night and my horniness. Benjamin.

One of the cats meows and Ryker bends down to talk to the ginger male. The other cat has disappeared, probably scouting the area or getting reinforcements. Ryker can still communicate with them even though he's shifted. It goes way beyond the rudimental form of communication I have with cats. He understands every single word, not just their intentions. I'm kind of jealous of that, but it makes sense, he's lived with those cats all his life, and not only that, they've also accepted him as their leader.

"Bowen says there is no other way inside than via the front gate," he translates. "No holes in the wall, no windows on the roof. It's a new building and it shows. The other warehouses all have weaknesses to exploit, but this one has been built to be secure."

"I'd feared that," Gryphon admits. "If this building has siren security, that also means that there will be further guarding measures inside. This won't be as easy as the other house where we simply walked in. This is a fortress, even though it doesn't look that way."

Another scream, but it isn't Benjamin this time. Hopefully, it's his attacker.

I wish I had something to cut through the walls, but I don't have all my breaking-and-entering equipment with me. After all, we were only planning to look at the blue house and then maybe go to the pub. Kidnapping wasn't on our agenda at all.

"Can't be helped, let's go through the door," I say, grimacing at the thought of giving up any stealth advantage we might still have.

"My cats are bringing reinforcements," Ryker reports, stroking the ginger male's head in thanks.

"Can you sense how many people are inside?" Gryphon asks, but I shake my head.

"The walls are too thick, sorry. There are scents of

maybe two dozen different people out here, but they could be old. No idea how many are in there right now."

"Guess we're in for a surprise." He smirks. "I've got to say, I don't always like surprises. Especially when they involve my family."

I realise that Ryker hasn't shown any surprise about Gryphon's talk of sirens and family connections. That means Gryphon has filled in the others while I was recovering. Good, that means one less secret.

"Should one of us stay behind, just in case?" Ryker asks.

I've thought of that myself, but since we don't have the advantage of surprise, it might be better to attack at full strength.

"No, we stay together." I take a deep breath. "Let's kill some evil people."

CHAPTER TWELVE

Of course, the massive doors at the front of the warehouse are locked. There's no doorbell either. That would have been kind of fun. Instead, I knock as loud as I can. The sound reverberates across the metal building, echoing far.

Heavy footsteps approach, three people. Let's hope they're not zombie mutants again. Although, killing them would distract me from the urge I feel to pull my two men closer to me, to touch them in all the right places. I'm starting to get distracted and that's a bad sign. Benjamin is in danger, he might be hurt, and here I am, fantasising about seeing these guys naked and on top of me.

A tiny hole opens in the door on the right and an eye blinks at us.

"Whaddaya want?"

I smile innocently. "We're doing a survey about how happy local businesses are with the services the council is providing. Would you like to answer a few of our questions?"

Blink. Blink.

The man steps away from the hole and another takes his place. A blue eye this time, with purple swelling just underneath.

"Of course, we'd love to help you with your survey," he says pleasantly, his voice a warm baritone. Gryphon clears his throat, confirming my suspicions. He's a siren. That means the Pack is involved. It doesn't surprise me, but the presence of one of their leaders makes me realise that this warehouse might be more important than I thought. Which also begs the question of why they brought Benjamin here. They must have expected us to follow our friend's scent.

It's a trap.

Of course it is. Question is, how quickly can we spring it before wiggling out of its grasp and turning the tables?

The man steps back from the peek hole and starts unlocking the door.

"Play along," Gryphon whispers. "Pretend to be under his influence."

I'm not sure how much good that will do. If this is a trap, this siren knows who and what I am. If they've been watching me, they might even know about Ryker and Gryphon. We don't have an advantage anymore, but maybe we can be unpredictable enough to make it all work out.

The double doors open with an irritating squeak.

They could do with some oiling. It's more a gate than a door, big enough for carts to pass through.

Three men await us. Two are giants, probably the same undying mutants we've already encountered, and one slim, well-dressed man between them. His goatee is precise and immaculate, his teeth a shiny white and his suit freshly pressed. The only thing that's not perfect about him is the large bruise under his left eye. It's fresh, maybe a couple of hours old, although since sirens heal slightly faster than humans, it might be more recent.

"Do come in," he says pleasantly. "How long will this take?"

It's impressive how he simply plays along with our ruse. I know that he knows that we're not what we're pretending to be. He knows that I know that he's got our friend. And yet, we play our roles, acting a scene where neither of us knows how it will end. It's kind of fun, in a way. Most of the people I kill are either stupid or too surprised to make it very entertaining. This, however, is new. The game is afoot and, despite the danger, I'm loving it.

He turns and walks to a couple of fancy looking chairs in the corner of this reception room. We follow and the two burly men fall in behind us, closing the door. We're trapped. Intentionally.

"Please sit down," he says in his enchanting voice. "Would you like something to drink?"

No thanks, I don't fancy being poisoned.

"We're good," I tell him with a wide smile. "This won't take long."

"No, I think it won't," he replies smugly. Something

presses against my back and I whirl around, but before I can even see how someone's touching me despite the two grunts being several feet away, my brain short-circuits and I collapse to the floor.

REGAINING CONSCIOUSNESS IS A LONG AND PAINFUL affair. My limbs are heavy and unresponsive, my brain a mess of scrambled thoughts. What the fuck happened? How did they take us down that easily? I'd made sure to keep a distance from both the siren and the men behind us. They didn't have weapons, not that I could see. Nothing long enough to poke us from behind, anyway. Whatever they did is something I've not encountered before.

Slowly, the lethargy leaves my limbs and I manage to open my eyes and sit up. I'm in a small room, by myself, and utterly naked. Urgh. Seriously? This is so textbook.

I check my hair. They even removed the lockpicks I'd used to tie it up in a bun. They knew what they were doing. Double urgh.

I stagger to my feet, glad they haven't chained me up like they did to Lily and Bethany. The walls are painted white, just like the door, the floor and the ceiling. The only non-white bit is a small chrome drain in the centre of the room. It feels a bit like a lab.

My heart starts beating faster. Please, no. Not a lab. I can deal with being tortured, but not being experimented on.

The door doesn't budge when I press against it.

Well, it was worth a try. There's a latch at the bottom of it, probably to push food in. My stomach growls at the thought. How long have I been here? It must have been a while; I wasn't hungry in the slightest when I entered the warehouse.

I sit down and concentrate on my cat senses. Nothing. Not a sound, not a scent, except for the sharp smell of antiseptics.

They've been thorough. As if they know precisely how to unsettle me.

Life is full of sounds, smells and tastes. If you're a shifter, even more so. I rely on my senses more than humans. Every second of the day, my mind catalogues new sensations and alerts me to anything that needs investigating. To be without any scents, any sounds at all, is terrifying.

I focus on my heartbeat, trying to find peace in the regular rhythm. It's too fast, though. I'm not quite scared enough to make it beat this fast, so that means whatever they did to me earlier has had an effect on my circulatory system.

I take a deep breath, in and out, keeping my mind on my breathing. It helps a little with the absence of other stimulants for my senses. I keep thinking of Gryphon, Ryker and Benjamin, but I try hard to stay away from those thoughts. They only make things worse. I'm sure the guys can handle themselves. If this is the Pack, they'll be far more interested in me than in the men.

The one thing I'm glad about is that Doctor Grandma is dead. The woman who created me, who created my siblings. It's a small relief, but it's better than nothing. She's not going to be able to hurt me. Other people can't be as bad as her, right?

THEY LEAVE ME IN THAT ROOM FOR WHAT FEELS LIKE AT least a day. My throat is parched, my stomach has given up growling, and my eyes are dropping with tiredness. I don't allow myself to sleep, though. I need to stay awake, ready to attack whoever enters my room. I need to escape, need to get out of here and free Benjamin. That's the whole point why I'm here.

I shift position for the hundredth time. The floor is cold and hard, but somehow I keep hoping that another spot on it might be a little comfier. I'd be more comfortable if I shifted, but I don't want to spend energy on that. Besides, I'm better at escaping as a human. My panther is strong and dangerous, but not good at being subtle when killing people.

How long are they going to keep me waiting? Until I fall asleep? Until I'm too weak to put up much resistance. Well, they're going to have to wait for a while. I'm not giving in that easily.

Seconds pass like hours. Minutes like days. I'm tired, I'm hungry, I'm fed up with being here. Now would be a good time for someone to break me out of here. But since I don't really think anyone will do that, I shall have to break myself out. Once they open this door, obviously. And then I'm going to free Benjamin and the guys, and take revenge on our captors, starting with that siren.

My eyes are itching with sleepiness. I start walking around my cell, counting the steps. Then I walk backwards and see if my count matches. Then I walk on my hands. And do some stretches. And punch the air imagining that it's the siren.

By the end of my workout, I'm a tiny bit less tired, but also a lot more exhausted. All I want is to curl up and sleep. But no, I can't do that. Need to stay awake. Need to be ready to fight.

There are no windows and I don't wear a watch, but my inner clock is pretty accurate. Thirty-one hours, it tells me. No wonder I'm ready to drink a river full of water followed by eating a pig or two. When I was still with the Pack, I was used to going for long times without food, but now, I've become used to regular meals and as much as I want to eat. I guess I've grown soft.

The air in this small room is starting to get stuffy. There's no vent to let in fresh air except for the tiny gap underneath the door. The drain isn't any use either. It carries a miniscule trickle of murky water, but I've not managed to pry off the grate. I've relieved myself over it once, but since I've not had any fluids, I've not had to go more than that one time. Hopefully, my intestines take pity on me and don't make me do a number two in here.

I can't suppress a yawn. When are they finally going to come to torture me?

"I'm bored!" I shout as loud as I can. My throat hurts from lack of water, but that can't be helped.

Nobody replies. Of course not. By now I've figured

out that this room is completely soundproof, neither letting sounds in nor out. All I can hear is my own heartbeat and breathing. As I said, I'm bored.

I only realise that I've fallen asleep when the door opens. I jump up, a little unsteady on my feet. How long has it been? Did I sleep for long? Fuck, I shouldn't have let myself do that. I was supposed to stay awake.

The siren enters, flanked by his two guards. One of them is holding a long silver rod, with a strange flickering light on its end. It must be some sort of weapon, but not like any I've ever seen before.

"Do sit down," the siren says in his soft, melodic voice. "You look like you're about to keel over."

I glare at him and stay standing, but I take one step back so I can lean against the wall.

He shrugs. "Suit yourself. I won't stay long anyway."

He rummages in his suit pocket and pulls out a crumpled piece of paper. "K1," he reads. "Termination has been recommended multiple times, but it has been kept alive as a control subject for now. K1 refuses to comply with her training. Measures will have to be taken." He looks up to observe my reaction. "Measures... what were those?"

I don't reply.

He shrugs and continues. "With age, K1 is becoming more rebellious. Her self-awareness is also increasing. It is no longer safe to keep her in proximity with the other clones. D.G. recommends exposing her to a new experiment to test K1's independence and problem-solving. Termination may be approved should said experiment fail."

A shiver runs down my back. He keeps saying that word. Termination. Killing me. Is that what he's about to do? It's kind of disappointing. He could have done that while I was unconscious.

"Do you know what experiment I'm talking about?"

His eyes are cold as they fix on my face, looking for any kind of emotion that I may show. Well, he's in for disappointment. I'm good at hiding what I feel. Even though my insides are clenched with fear. Because I have no idea what experiment he's on about. I don't remember ever being part of an experiment while I was at the Pack. Yes, sometimes they'd take some blood and measure my reactions, but I don't think that's what he's talking about.

"I'm afraid that this is the end of the experiment," the man says with a smile that might be interpreted as kind if his eyes weren't so cold. "We cannot let it continue, not after the little stunt you pulled at the research facility."

I'm having trouble following what he's saying. He's talking as if there's an experiment just now... but all they've done is put me in an empty room and let me stew in my own thoughts for a while. Not exactly very dramatic.

"Professor Lakefield had high hopes that you might eventually succeed in showing your full potential, but now that he's gone and I'm the one in charge, I think it's time to stop being sentimental and simply end this process."

Lakefield... Gryphon mentioned him. The man who trained Grandma Doctor, the one who was involved in setting up the cloning. So he's gone? That's good news, right? Him and Grandma Doctor both being out of the picture should make me feel relieved, but having this new guy staring at me as if I'm a lab rat is not exactly making me happy.

"Then why am I still alive?" I ask, my voice almost too hoarse to be heard. "If you want to kill me, you've had enough chances to do so."

"Trust me, you'd be dead already if I didn't need you as insurance."

I shoot him a questioning glance. I hate that I don't get what he's talking about. I need more information, but he's the only one who can provide me with it.

"I was rather surprised to find a siren in your employ, especially one of such pedigree. He's refusing to cooperate right now, which is the only reason why you're still alive. Hurting you a little might make him come to his senses."

He gestures to one of the men behind him, who pulls out a camera and points it at me.

"Please try and scream a little," the siren says with a smile and steps aside, letting the man with the silver rod approach me. I move away from him, but the room is too small to let me evade him and besides, I'm too weak to show much resistance.

"Wait, how do I switch this thing on?" the guy with the camera asks. I guess these men weren't chosen because of their intelligence.

While the siren grunts in annoyance and shows him how to press a button, I keep my eyes fixed on the man with the rod. The light at the end seems to ebb brighter in waves as if the electricity inside of it is fluctuating. Curious. It looks pretty, but not pretty enough to want to touch it. Who knows, this could be the same weapon they used to knock me unconscious.

The click of the camera makes me whirl around. Stupid instincts.

The movement is too much, my legs buckle, I trip, fall, end up on the floor. My naked skin protests at the sudden contact, but then the rod is pressed into my side and pain is all I feel.

I scream, my voice sucked up by the soundproof room, and somehow that makes the pain so much worse. Nobody can hear me scream. I'm alone, in pain, and they're using this very fact to hurt Gryphon.

I curl into a ball, barely hanging on to consciousness.

Something hits my thigh, hard and painful. It's the last drop of water in my barrel of pain. Darkness welcomes me and I let it embrace me.

CHAPTER THIRTEEN

Cold water kisses my skin and I come to life, staring at my surroundings with wide, itchy eyes. Two legs close to me, ready to be attacked. Except that my body isn't cooperating. Just like before, I'm paralysed, and I can't even evade the icy water that is being poured over me. I just about manage to turn my head to avoid it hitting my nose and mouth, but the rest of me isn't so lucky. The cold seeps into my bones and shivers start making me tremble. Wasn't the rod-poking enough? Do they now have to resort to this?

"Now you can drink," the man chuckles darkly and steps away. The door falls shut behind him, leaving me alone in my white, empty room.

I hear the water trickle towards the drain. It's going to be all gone soon. I need to drink, I need fluids to keep functioning. I try to turn, to let my tongue touch the floor, but my body is refusing to budge. All I can do is lie there, listening as the water disappears, increasing my thirst with every drop falling down the drain.

Nobody comes to see me again. No more water, no more strange talk of experiments. I let myself drift, no longer caring about what's happening to me. If I'm really a bargaining chip for making Gryphon do what they want, they're going to have to keep me alive. That's what I'm telling myself. They won't let me die, they can't.

Right?

My stomach has knotted itself into a ball. My hunger has disappeared, leaving behind a strange emptiness. I'm still thirsty, though. The water on my skin has dried. I wish I had some sort of amphibian shifter powers that would allow me to soak up water through my skin.

When someone finally opens the door again, I don't even look up. I need to preserve my strength. Not that I've got enough to escape, but I might be able to land a single hit on that siren's nose. It would be satisfying, even if it was the last thing I did. Going out with a bang and a bit of blood.

A bowl is placed near my head, then the footsteps walk away from me once more and the door is closed. I sniff. Food. Nothing special, some oats and water, but it's the first meal I've had in over two days so I don't really care. I push myself up until I'm sitting against the wall and start slurping the gruel. It's absolutely tasteless. The siren's cook should be fired. At least it doesn't taste of any poison that I know of. As I said, they don't want me dead - yet.

It takes my throat a while to open up enough to let some food through. I wish there was more water in the porridge. Dying of thirst is much easier than dying of hunger. I could still live a few days without food, but not without water. My body is that of a shifter and I use up a lot more energy than humans. I need to be fed regularly to keep up my strength.

When I'm done, I lick the bowl clean, not wasting a single drop. This might be the difference between life and death. And I'm a survivor.

I lean back, turning the bowl in my hands. It's not heavy enough to be used as a weapon, but that won't stop me from trying.

I will get out of here, one way or another.

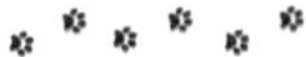

FOUR DAYS. EIGHT BOWLS OF TASTELESS PORRIDGE. FOUR bottles of water. One very bored Kat.

Time passes slowly and without pity. The siren doesn't come to visit me again. My food is brought by one of his lackeys, but they never talk to me.

They're not letting me starve, but they're also not giving me enough food to let me keep my strength. I'm growing weaker every day, even though I'm trying to keep myself busy with exercises, shadow boxing and random shouting matches with the walls. I rub my knuckles. Yesterday I punched the door in a moment of desperate madness. It didn't budge, obviously, and I didn't feel any better after. With me being so weak, my body is taking its time to heal the bruising.

I scratch the back of my neck. I need a shower. My hair is oily and dry at the same time, while my armpits are starting to give off a decidedly yucky smell. Maybe it would be better if I shifted and used my long cat tongue to lick myself clean, but I'm not sure I would even survive a shift in my current condition. It would need too much energy.

The door clicks open without warning. This is too early for more food. They've been delivering it always at the same times, every twelve hours. Not even four hours have passed since the last visit, so this must be something else.

I scramble to my feet, the bowl in my hand. I might just throw it at whoever comes in. Just to make me feel better.

It's the siren. One of his men puts a chair in the centre of the room, then joins his comrade by the door, making sure I don't escape. As if I could.

The siren sits down on the chair, crosses his legs and purses his fingers beneath his chin. Textbook villain. Do they teach that kind of behaviour somewhere? Is there a Villain Academy?

"You don't look too good," he observes, his eyes running over my body.

"And whose fault is that?" I spit, glad my voice isn't quite as hoarse today.

He shrugs. "You should be grateful that I'm feeding you at all. If this were up to just me, you'd be a corpse drifting in the river by now."

So he's not the one in charge, or at least not the only one. That's good to know.

"Our mutual friend insists on proof of life, so please smile for the camera."

One of the brutes has his camera pointed at me once again, but at least this time, they're not using the metal rod on me. I'm tempted to cover my nakedness with my hands, but it's not like they've had ample chance to stare at me for the past couple of days. By now, I'm not really bothered about my clothes being gone. What I would like is a blanket to hide under.

"I've been told it was a mistake to interrupt the experiment, but it can't be helped now. We have ways to make you forget, and we've used those on you too many times to count, but this time, there are other people involved. Your friends have been searching for you. Even if I make you forget, I can't do that to every single cat in this town."

They're searching for me, the cats. Hopefully, Lennox, Lily and Bethany too, if they all made it back to our home in one piece. I hope he hasn't hurt Benjamin. The thief is human, so he won't be of much use to the Pack. I doubt they needed him for anything more than a lure to get us here. Hopefully, that doesn't mean that they see him as expendable.

Gryphon still seems to be in captivity, but has Ryker managed to escape to mobilise his cats? I really hope so. That would mean two of my men are safe.

When he doesn't continue, I take the initiative. "What happens now?"

He smirks. "The two of us are going to have a chat."

"Aren't we doing that just now?"

His grin widens. "No, we're not. Not the kind of chat I'm planning to have with you."

"You'll have to be more clear."

I try and seem as confident as I possibly can, but the slight quiver in my legs betrays me.

"We're going to go to the lab and have our chat there. Like we always used to. Oh, but you can't remember that, can you."

It's not a question. He knows that I can't remember. If this ever actually happened. Which I doubt.

"I've never seen you before," I snarl from between clenched teeth.

"But you have," he replies cheerily. "You always call me such lovely names. Quite the wildcat, aren't you. I'm going to miss our little chats. They were always so much fun."

It's hard to hide my confusion. I have no idea what he's on about.

He waves one of his guards forward, who's suddenly wielding that silver rod again. Fuck, no.

"I'll follow you," I say quickly. "No need for that."

I don't think his grin could get any wider. "Oh, but I love to hear you scream."

He nods at the grunt and before I can even brace myself, the rod is slammed against my ribs and pain is all I can feel.

THIS IS BECOMING A FRUSTRATING TRADITION. WAKING unable to move, the taste of blood in my mouth, the memory of pain still fresh in my mind. Except that this time, I'm not in my cell. I'm on a chair, my arms and legs strapped to it with thick leather bands. I dimly remember seeing such a chair at the Pack research building, but since we burned down that building, this has to be somewhere else. There are no windows in this room, and just like my cell, it seems to be soundproof, meaning I have no idea where I am. For all I know, I could still be in the warehouse.

I'm alone in the room. At least that gives me the chance to look around while my body is still recovering from the paralysis. It's a lab, there's no doubt about that. We've got some of the instruments lying on tables and shelves in our Meow lab, but a lot of them I don't recognise. Two large metal tables are to my right, while to my left is a desk and the door leading to freedom. The lights above me are bright and harsh, making my skin look pale and sickly. Or maybe that's what my skin actually looks like just now.

I guess I should be glad that there's no blood splatters on the floor or dissected body parts in glass jars. This lab is clean and tidy, not looking like they're regularly murdering cat shifters in here. Maybe I'll be the first.

After some compulsory struggling against my bonds, I lay back and wait.

I'm bored by the time the door finally opens and the siren enters. I realise I still don't know his name. But then, I don't really care. I won't send him a thank you card any time soon.

"I hope you're comfortable?" he asks with a fake smile and takes a seat on a high back desk chair. He almost makes it look like a throne.

"Do you recognise this room?"

I don't reply.

"I take that as a no. Curious how well the conditioning still works. Some of us - not me though - thought you'd start to remember as soon as you were no longer subjected to our stimuli, but it seems they were wrong. I'm rather glad about this. It means I can surprise you."

"Surprise me with what?"

"The truth." He clucks his tongue. "But I think we should do some tests first. You won't be happy to do them after I've told you everything."

"I'm not happy now either," I growl.

He ignores me and gets up from his chair. He rummages in one of the desk drawers until he finds a couple of photos. They're old, their corners yellowed. He waves one of them in my face.

"Do you recognise her?"

It's a woman wearing a lab coat, her hair held in a tight knot on top of her head. She looks angry and very familiar. A young version of Grandma Doctor. I'm not going to say that name out loud though. It seems wrong to call her such an innocent thing. I rake my mind for her actual name, the one Gryphon told me. Jane? Jasmin? Something with a J... and then Fitzroy.

"Doctor Fitzroy?" I ask, mostly because I'm curious and want to explain what's going on. If he wants to give me information, then I'll gladly accept it. Every titbit might help me in bringing down the Pack.

"Very good. What about him?"

The next photograph shows a young man, also in a lab coat, with thick glasses and a strangely blank face.

"No idea."

"Curious," he mutters, but doesn't comment any further.

"Him?"

Another young man that I don't recognise. I shake my head.

"How about her?"

He shows me a picture of myself, sitting on a bench on a sunny day.

"Very funny."

He doesn't smile. "Look closer."

I frown and focus back on the picture. The clothes... I'm not sure I own a pair of jeans like that. And her hair is longer than mine. There is a certain sadness around her eyes, thin lines that aren't on my face.

This isn't me.

I want to reach for the picture, but I'm bound to the chair. Frustrated, I lean forward as much as I can.

The woman on the photo can't be one of the clones. She's as old as I am now, or maybe a few years older. Since all my clones are younger than me, that means she's...

"The original," the siren whispers dramatically, confirming my suspicions. "The template for you and all the other K-subjects."

I can't look away from the picture. That's me and yet not me. With Little Kat, it was different. She's a younger version of myself, but when I look at her, I don't see me like I am now. I probably looked like her when I was her age, but I can't remember. It's not like you memorise whatever you look like every time you stare into your face in a mirror.

"This was taken on the day we created you. Your birthday, so to speak. It was always our goal to have you reach the same age as your original, to then compare the measurements we took on that day twenty-two years ago. Sadly, I don't think you're going to survive that long."

He actually looks a little disappointed.

"If you want the data, why not let me live?"

"You wouldn't like that. What you've experienced in the past few days is only a small taste of what your future here would be like. You should call yourself lucky if I release you from your pain soon."

How very ominous.

I growl at him. "How about you don't inflict any pain on me and I'll let you live?"

"I'm afraid that's not possible. If you hadn't destroyed one of our research facilities, I might be able to keep you alive for a little longer, but now, you've proved that you can be too dangerous and unpredictable. We always assumed you'd one day start attacking the Pack, but we didn't expect you to gather allies to help you. All K-subjects were raised to be self-sufficient and without personal relationships, so I have to say, we were all rather surprised by that. Finding employees, making friends, getting others to fight on your side, those are all highly unusual behaviours for one of your kind."

He's wrong. Little Kat loves the company of others. I might not be a very social person but I can appreciate cooperating with others to achieve a goal. Who am I kidding, I do like having my Meow folks around. They're my friends, even though it still surprised me how they turned into that. It's not like I ever really tried to be their friend. It just happened.

He pulls another picture from the stack and shows it to me. An elderly man with a top hat and scars on his face, a man I recognise immediately. Mystery Man, the guy who made Meow possible. Who gave me money. Who left me his house in his will. Who I thought was an enemy of the Pack.

"You look like you recognise Professor Lakefield. Say hello to your creator."

I stare at the siren as my world crumbles into dust.

CHAPTER FOURTEEN

The physical pain they've caused me is nothing compared to the mental pain I feel tearing at my heart just now. It's all been a lie. Mystery Man, my benefactor, worked for the Pack. He *created* me. I was probably sent to him by his own orders. And I fell for it.

The siren is quiet, leaving me to my thoughts. He's rummaging around, and I'm pretty sure he's doing it on purpose. Letting the truth set in.

I've been betrayed.

I've never been free. I've never had the life I thought I had. It's all been engineered by the same man who created me in a lab. They sent me to kill him, but it was just a game. He'd always planned to set me free, but on his terms. They knew I was planning to escape, and to prevent that, they loosened the leash just enough for me to feel safe.

All those cases Mystery Man gave me, all those people I killed. He told me that some of them were part of the Pack, that their deaths would help get me closer to bringing them down. Now that I know who he was, I can only imagine who I killed. Probably people who were working against the Pack. And I assassinated them. I never stopped being their weapon.

Did he ever actually have a granddaughter? Did he really die and leave me the house? Or was that all part of the same game?

My life is a lie. My freedom an illusion. I'm just a puppet whose strings have been loosened for a moment, but they're still there, and now that I'm in the hands of the siren, the strings are taut again, ready to control me, make me dance for them.

Except that I'm done.

No more.

My options are clear. I can submit to him, let him kill me, or I can fight and take my life back. Forge it anew. And if I die in the process, then that's fine. At least I died fighting for my dreams.

No more.

I snarl at the siren. "It's not working."

He seems a little taken aback. "What do you mean?"

"You trying to break me. I know what you're doing, and it's not working. I don't care that I've been betrayed. I don't care that you let me escape. Because it's all been training for me. You've helped me become the person I am now. Someone who's not afraid."

He shrugs. "It doesn't matter what you think. What matters is that you're here now and that you're back under my control. I couldn't care less what you think in your final moments."

I smile at him. "But you do. You get off on it. I can

smell your arousal. You're a psychopath, you feed off hurting others. But you can't hurt me anymore. You've just told me the worst thing I could hear. Which means that now, there's nothing worse you can do. And here I am, smiling at you."

His mask slips. He's not as good as me at hiding his thoughts. He looks disappointed. Crestfallen.

I laugh. "You wanted this to be a victory, yet it's become your greatest failure. You thought this would break me, but, in fact, it's put me back together."

I feel strong. Stronger than ever before. Like a switch has been flicked inside of me, one I never even knew existed. I close my eyes and pull my cat to the surface. Not enough to shift, but enough to lend me her strength. Those bounds may be strong enough to hold a human, but they're no match for me.

Raw power is cursing through my veins. I lift my right arm and the leather cuff rips open.

The siren staggers back, his eyes wide. Bet he didn't expect this to happen. He probably regrets that he didn't take his goons in here with him. He's alone with me, with a rabid shifter thirsting for revenge.

He tries to get away, but I'm too fast. My fingernails turn to claws and make quick work of the remaining bonds. I'm free and ready to kill.

With a snarl, I jump, reaching the siren just before his hand touches the doorknob. We tumble to the ground, me on his back, and then my teeth are at his neck. He stinks of fear. Gryphon was right, sirens pull the strings but rarely get their hands dirty. This man is likely not wearing a single weapon.

"Remember this," I hiss into his ear. "You made me. You did this to yourself."

And then I shift and rip out his throat.

I leave a trail of blood in my wake. The siren was only the first. I tore open the first grunt's belly, watching as he tried to keep his intestines inside of him. I let him struggle, leaving him to a long and painful death. I doubt even his healing powers are strong enough to restore that much damage. The second man tried to stab me with his silver rod, but I ripped off his head before he could touch me. Two others waited for me at the top of the stairs. I slashed open their throats, enjoying their gurgling sounds as they cursed me with their dying breath.

I'm covered in blood, none of it mine. I'm a killer and I've only just begun.

The house is empty now, but I smell other humans nearby, and among their scents, Ryker. I don't bother with the door. Instead, I jump out of a window, ignoring the small cuts of glass against my skin. The scent leads me to the neighbouring house, painted a bright blue. Three men and one woman meet me in the garden, brandishing swords and more of the metal rods, but they're no challenge to me. I rip them apart and don't mind the taste of blood at all. The woman's blood is sweet; she's not quite human. Just like what Little Kat described. I feel like I want more of it, drink my fill, but other humans are preparing to fight me, and I need to make sure none of them hurt my Ryker.

I barge into the house through the open door. Thanks for leaving that open, dead people. The hallway is narrow, letting only one of the humans attack me at a time. The house is full of them, at least fifteen, although some of them might be those mutants whose scent I can't tell apart from humans. Even better. The more of them I kill, the fewer can hurt people I like.

Three, four, they all die. One of them manages to nip my skin with his dagger, but I barely feel it. My large paws step onto their corpses, my claws sinking into dead flesh. It's a pity my fur is black, it doesn't show the blood as nicely as Lennox's white fur would.

I sniff the air. Ryker is down below, probably held in the basement just like I was in the other house. Maybe he's even got the same cell. I growl at the thought of my proud cat being imprisoned. Starved. Maybe even tortured.

That mental image makes me rear up and race down the stairs. There a giant man waiting at the bottom of the steps, brandishing two axes at once. He may have been a challenge before, but not anymore. I jump, twisting in the air to avoid his blades, then wrap my jaws around his neck and bite. He sinks to the ground, his body twitching. Knowing that he's one of the mutants – the size of him kind of gives it away – I tear off his head, kicking it down the corridor like a ball.

A polished black shoe stops it, pressing it down onto the floor. I look up at the man stopping my game. Another siren. He seems vaguely familiar, with his pale blond mop of hair and turgid face. A smirk curves his lips as if he's enjoying the carnage I have wrought.

"You should stop now," he says in a soft voice, reminding me of the other siren. "You wouldn't want me to hurt your friend."

His accent is posh and I could easily imagine him as a politician, controlling the humans of this town.

I snarl at him, ready to tear out his throat. I love doing that. The spray of blood, the gurgling sound, the fear in their eyes as they realise that there's no way back from this.

A whimpered meow makes me back down. Ryker. He's in pain.

Foam starts to build around my fangs. They hurt him. They're all going to die.

"One step further and they will kill him."

He could be bluffing, but even in my frenzied state, I'm scared to risk that.

I stop, my body tense, ready to spring into action as soon as I think it's safe. Not safe for me, but for Ryker.

"How did you escape?" he asks me, even though he must be aware that I can't answer while I'm shifted. "No matter, I've got you now. And I should be glad you've killed David, he was getting a pain in the arse."

I growl. He doesn't have me. I won't submit to him. I'm just biding my time until I know that Ryker isn't in immediate danger.

My senses tell me that there are two humans with Ryker in a room not far from here. It can't be the same soundproof room I was kept in since I can hear their heartbeats and smell their sweat. They're scared. How lovely. That's going to make this even more fun. It's always more entertaining when your prey is panicked before it dies.

All that stands between them and me is this turd-faced blond wretch.

But not for much longer.

I growl once again, pleased that his heartbeat increases a little. He's not as calm as he makes out to be. He's right to be scared. I'm *so* close to biting off his dick.

"Shift back," he commands. "Then we can talk about what to do next."

I flash my sharp teeth at him instead. No chance am I shifting. I've never felt so alive, so *right* as a panther. This is the real me, the real Kat.

Footsteps approach from behind him and a moment later, one of his guards turns around the corner. He's the biggest one yet, so broad his shoulders touch the walls of the corridor. How does he find clothes that fit him?

"Do you need any assistance, sir?" he asks in a deep, burly voice. He sounds surprisingly intelligent for one of those brutes.

"Yes, stay here. This little kitten is trying to show me her claws."

Did this fucker just call me a kitten?

I lunge, no longer thinking straight. My claws rake across his face, ripping out one of his eyes in the process. With my hind legs, I push against the big man, just about managing to have him stumble back. He's too strong to be brought down, but it gives me enough time to bring my jaws around the blond man's throat and squeeze them shut.

I need to be fast now, Ryker might be in danger. I launch myself at the big man, but suddenly he pulls a knife from somewhere and holds it out. I can't stop myself in time and it slices into my abdomen.

I howl in pain, but it's only a dim echo of the strangled sound the man makes when I push my left hind paw into his groin and extend my claws as far as I can. This time, he goes down, landing on his back, grunting at the impact. Then I rip my claws down and all he can do is scream as I sever his cock from his miserable body.

For good measure, I also bite his throat and slice open his stomach, then step away to inspect my own wound. It's deep, but it doesn't seem to have hit any vital organs. It's bleeding a lot, but it will heal. Nothing I can do much about right now. Staying in my panther body will help; I heal faster like this.

The wound slows me down, but not enough to stop me entirely. I grit my teeth, ignoring the pain as much as possible, and follow Ryker's scent. There's one human with him. Even injured, that shouldn't be a problem. On the contrary, I'm looking forward to my next kill. My thirst for revenge isn't nearly sated yet. There will be more deaths, lots of them.

As soon as I round a corner, a skinny man runs at me, brandishing two curved knives. How disappointing, he's not even one of those brutes. He looks entirely human and smells like it, too. Blood is coating his hands, but it's not human blood. My heart beats faster. This man has hurt Ryker. I'm going to hurt him so much.

I launch myself at him, trying not to focus on the

stinging pain in my abdomen. I hate being wounded. Luckily, it doesn't happen very often.

He's fast, evading me by dropping to the ground and executing an elegant backwards roll. He jumps into a crouch, his knives pointing at me. Call me impressed. Not enough to let him live though. With a growl, I jump at him again, holding out one paw to deflect his attacks while using the other to strike. He turns to his right, but not fast enough to escape my sharp claws. They rake through his clothes and tear into his skin, cutting through one of his nipples in the process. I feel a little guilty about that. I wouldn't want anyone to cut my nipples in half.

The man screams and I use his momentary distraction to embed my claws deep into his chest. He feebly tries to lift his knives, but it's too late. I rip open his chest, exposing his heart. It takes one last beat, a contraction of the body's most beautiful muscle, then it shudders to a stop. The man is dead and I'm fighting the urge to eat his heart.

Fuck, I need to focus on my human side. I'm turning too feral.

But then I hear Ryker scream and all those thoughts go out of the window.

He needs me, not the human but the predator in me, and I'm going to save him.

CHAPTER FIFTEEN

Ryker's cell isn't quite as white as my own was. His walls are a pale grey, and he's even got a bucket, not just a drain. Luxury.

The downside is that he's chained to the floor by a thick iron chain. Very medieval. They've put a collar around his neck, but I sigh in relief when I see it's not one of the mind control collars. This one seems to be just normal metal, wrapped around his throat to keep him in check. He's also got bronze cuffs around his wrists. I recognise those. They prevent you from shifting. I wonder why they never put those on me. Maybe by starving me, they knew I'd be too weak to shift. Well, until they broke me and crushed the barrier that was keeping me from gaining my full strength. That isn't to say that I'm not hungry, but at least I won't collapse any time soon.

Ryker is curled up on the floor, but his heartbeat is steady. He's alive. Hopefully just unconscious.

I bump my head against his back. He groans. His

eyelids flutter open, but he seems too exhausted to keep them open for long. What have they done to him? He screamed in pain not long ago. Maybe it was one of those rods. That would explain why he's so drowsy. Poor kitty. But how the heck am I going to get him out of here? He's too heavy to carry. If he was shifted, I could carry him by the scruff of his neck like a mother panther does with her cubs. For that, I'd need to get his cuffs off first though and there's no way I'm going to achieve that unless I turn human. That's too dangerous, though. Who knows what state I'll be in once I shift.

I hate to admit it, but what I need is help.

"I'm going to come back," I meow at Ryker. His mouth twitches as if he's trying to reply, but he's too weak to speak. If I hadn't already killed everyone in this house, I'd do it all over again.

I rub my nose against his skin one more time, then turn and run upstairs and out into the garden. Bloody corpses stare at me accusingly. I kick one of them in retribution, before meowing as loud as I can, calling for any cats in the vicinity.

It only takes thirty seconds before one shows up, a grey tabby with a missing ear. He inclines his head when he approaches me. How very polite. I like him.

"Are you one of Ryker's?" I ask, not wasting time on introductions.

"I'm not, but I know cats who are. How can I be of assistance?"

Curious, a cat who isn't part of Ryker's family. I wonder what stopped him from joining. Maybe he's a loner. Hopefully, he's trustworthy.

"I need you to find some of Ryker's cats and tell them to get Kat's humans. They'll know what that means. And tell them to hurry."

"What's in it for me?"

Urgh. Cats.

"A month's supply of catnip," I concede grudgingly.

"Deal."

"Hurry," I remind him. "This is important."

The tabby nods and jumps off. I really, really hope he's going to do his job.

While waiting, I stake out the area. There are a few humans in the neighbouring buildings, but none of them is Benjamin, and they don't smell like they've ever been in contact with the people I killed. As much as my thirst for blood pushes me to kill them all, kill every single human in this street, my desire to protect Ryker and stay close to him wins.

I explore the house, hoping to catch a whiff of Gryphon's scent. I've found Ryker, but my siren is still missing. He must be alive though, from what the other siren said. As soon as I've got Ryker to a place of safety, I'm going to search for Gryphon.

A place of safety. I huff and shaky my body, ruffling my fur. The Meow headquarters will no longer feel safe. They're part of the setup, the lie that made me believe that I had a home of my own. Not anymore. Pack money paid for that house, which means I don't want it. I know there are no bugs in there; I checked for that when I first moved in. That doesn't mean that we're not under surveillance. And who knows what kind of surprises they've hidden in the building. If I were them,

I'd add a way to end the experiment if it was to fail. Like explosives underneath the house. Let's hope they didn't think like that, but I lived with the Pack for long enough to know that's precisely what they'd do.

As soon as Ryker is conscious again, we're going to have to get our belongings and find a new home. My chest aches at the thought. For the first time in my life, I'd had a home. A place I felt safe. One I'd made into my own little assassin headquarters.

They've taken that from me.

As if it's not enough to know truths that broke my heart. They also had to take my home.

With no sign of any cats, I return to the basement and snuggle against Ryker. He groans softly, but he's still not able to talk. I wrap my body around him protectively, hoping he'll be able to feel my presence.

"You're safe now," I whisper as quietly as a panther can. "I'm going to make sure they'll never hurt us again."

And I will. I'm going to find us a new home. I'm going to destroy the Pack. And I'm going to save my sisters.

BY THE TIME THE OTHERS ARRIVE, RYKER HAS STARTED to stir. I don't feel like moving at all. My belly hurts; the wound isn't healing fast enough. If any of the Pack people came back, I'd have a hard time defending us. Luckily though, I recognise my team's scents before they make it down into the basement.

Before I can even turn, Lennox has me in his arms, holding me tight. He runs his fingers through my fur, telling me through touch alone how much he's missed me.

Beth kneels by Ryker's side and starts examining the cat, while Lily adds one hand to Lennox's, stroking me. Her other arm is in a cast, so I guess it must be broken.

"You're hurt," she mutters. "That looks bad."

It feels bad, too. It should be less inflamed by now, but I think it's getting worse. I hope there wasn't any poison on the blades. I didn't smell any, but I'm beginning to realise that doesn't mean anything. The Pack has aces up their sleeves that I have no idea about. Like the mutant humans who smell human but have abilities only shifters should have.

"Is Gryphon here too?" Lily asks. I tiredly shake my head. Lennox uses that moment to lift my head into his lap, scratching me behind the ears just the way I like it.

"At least we have the two of you back," Lennox says, his voice strangely choked. Is he emotional? Aww. My wolf missed me.

"He seems fine, just exhausted," Beth reports, having finished her examination of Ryker. "But we should get you out of here soon so that you can recover. We only have one problem with that…"

I look at her properly for the first time. Something's changed, and I doubt it was intentional. Getting a haircut while your friends are missing is something I doubt even Bethany would do.

She grimaces when she notices me staring at her

hair. Half of it is missing. "Yeah, about that. We had a bit of a fire…"

I growl in frustration. The Pack attacked my home while I was held prisoner.

Lennox increases his ear scratching to calm me down. "The house is gone," he whispers. "We managed to get some things out before it all caught fire, but it's no longer habitable. We lost all the research Bethany has been doing on clones. Benjamin-"

I lift my head in surprise. Benjamin is with them?

"Yes, he managed to escape on his own," Lennox answers my unspoken question. "They underestimated him, thinking he's just a weak human. He made his way back to us three days ago. Right now, he's keeping guard at our new home."

I have so many questions, but I'm tired, so tired. I let my eyelids fall shut and doze, barely listening to my friends' voices around me. I need to regain my strength before I can shift and get out of here, but at least I've killed everyone who might try to hurt us.

At some point, Ryker is taken out of my arms. I struggle, instinctively wanting to keep him close, but Lennox's strong grip prevents me from doing anything.

"You need to shift," he whispers gently. "I can't carry you home otherwise."

I can walk, I try to say, but not even a simple meow leaves my lips. Pain shoots through my belly when I try to get up. And I've still got my eyes closed. Not a good way to do it. I let myself fall down to the hard ground again, hating the weakness that's suddenly weighing down my limbs. Not long ago, I was stronger than I'd ever been before. Now, I'm the opposite.

"Shift, Kat. Please, shift."

I can't. There's no energy to initiate the shift. That wound is sucking out all my energy, leaving me tired and paralysed. It must be poison. Hopefully, Bethany has an antidote. Oh no. The house burned down. Did she manage to get her supplies? What if she doesn't have any of her poisons and antidotes? That would be a hard blow to Meow, and maybe even a death sentence to me right now.

"What if we put the cuffs on her? Would that force her to shift back?"

No, I want to growl. That's a terrible idea.

But words are hard to form. I drift off, no longer aware of what is happening around me.

My last conscious thought is that this may have been my last thought, ever.

CHAPTER SIXTEEN

I wake sandwiched between two warm bodies. Almost too hot, but not quite enough to make me want to get up.

Instead of speaking and destroying this sweet moment of happiness, I simply lie there, listening to their heartbeats and enjoying their touch. I'm rather happy to be still alive. I no longer feel any pain in my abdomen, so it seems my body has either healed itself or has had some help from Bethany or someone else.

"You awake?" Ryker mutters sleepily.

"Mmmhmmmm."

That's as far as my vocal abilities go right now. I want to ask him how he feels, but I don't sense any distress or pain from him, and his breathing and heartbeat are nice and steady. He's alright. Thank the big fat cat in the sky.

"How are you feeling?" Lennox whispers from behind me. His hot breath strokes my neck in the most delicious way. Maybe I can entice him to lick me there.

And maybe do some more lovely things, as long as I don't have to move.

"Mmmhmmmm."

He chuckles. "I'll take that as meaning good. I'm glad you're back amongst the living."

"Mmmhm?"

"The blade you were stabbed with was poisoned. Luckily, Bethany had some antidotes here, but to carry you out of that house, Lily had to put those cuffs on you. They made you shift, but it didn't look very pleasant."

I try to remember, but it's all a hazy fog. That's probably a good thing. It sounds like it would have hurt, a lot.

"Anyway, we got the two of you back here, and then Bethany managed to get the poison out of your bloodstream. Your body was really cold though, so we volunteered to warm you up."

Ryker laughs softly. "It was such a terrible sacrifice."

I bet. I love the way their bodies perfectly mould against mine. The only thing missing is Gryphon.

"Where are we?" I mutter sleepily, my words slurred.

Lennox winces. "Our new home. For now, anyway. It's a wagon, a big one. Benjamin bought it from a circus performer that he knew. We thought it would be good to have a home that can be moved if needs be."

A bloody wagon. A few days ago, I was happily living in a big house, content and making plans to improve it. Now, we're practically homeless.

And it's all because of the Pack. I'm going to bring them down, taking them apart one by one. Ripping them to pieces. Making sure they know that it was me who brought their demise.

And then, I'm going to be happy. Safe. For the first time in my life, I'll feel properly safe. I got close to that feeling in my old house, but I was never entirely relaxed. There was always the danger that something might happen, that the Pack might come after me.

Now I know how right I was to fear them.

Lennox wraps an arm around my waist, pulling me even closer. "We're going to make this our home until we find somewhere better. And at least we're all together now."

"We're not. Gryphon isn't here."

The two men stay silent.

"What? Did he escape?"

"Kat," Ryker says softly and very carefully, as if he expects me to explode any moment now. "My cats have seen him. He was walking around near the Pack headquarters. Alone. Without guards. I'm sorry, but they said he didn't look like a prisoner."

"They must have been mistaken," I snap, sounding more aggressive than I would like to. They took pictures of me as proof of life. They were blackmailing him, forcing him to do whatever they want."

"Then why isn't he back yet?" Lennox asks, his voice neutral. "By now, he should know that you escaped. You killed over a dozen people, news of that would have spread quickly. If all they had as leverage on him was you, then he could have left by now."

"Maybe they imprisoned him as soon as they knew that I escaped. Maybe he's in a cell now, waiting for us to rescue him." I ball my fists, forcing myself to believe that. "Or maybe he's searching for us right now. He might be at the old house, not knowing where we are now. We should go back and leave a message for him. Make sure that he knows where to find us."

"My cats are monitoring the house," Ryker interrupts. "He's not been there. If he does come to the house, they'll lead him here, don't worry, but so far, he's not showed up."

"Then they have him locked up," I whisper. "We need to break him out."

Lennox clears his throat. "Kat, do you think there's a chance that Gryphon is part of it? One of them? That he's joined our group simply to spy on us?"

My stomach churns. No, I refuse to believe that. Not Gryphon. He's my friend, he's more than that. We've been naked together, we've explored each other inside out. I know him, and I know that he's not a traitor.

"No," is all I say. "No."

Neither of the guys replies and I kind of hate them for it. They should be reassuring me that Gryphon is indeed one of us, that he's not betrayed us, but their silence speaks of their doubts.

I sit up, leaving their reassuring warmth. "There's only one way to find out. We have to find him."

Ryker yawns and pulls the duvet closer. "Finding him isn't the problem, my cats have already done that. It's getting to him without being spotted. He's in their headquarters and they've increased their guards. There's no way of sneaking in that I can see."

I huff. "I'm not giving up on him just like that. I'm

going to find a way to contact him, you'll see. And I'll prove that he's not betrayed me. Not betrayed all of us."

I climb off the bed, which is really just a large mattress on the wooden floor of the wagon. There are windows on three sides of the room, all of them covered with dainty red curtains. A few built-in shelves and cubby holes are the only other furniture. I hope this isn't the only bedroom in our new home. I'm okay sharing with my men, but I'd rather not have my Meow employees here as well.

If they're going to stay here with me. The Pack won't be as interested in them as they are in me. If they left, they could probably have a good life. Start again. Maybe even create their own Meow 2.0.

A shiver runs through me at the thought. I'd miss them. A while ago, I'd never have admitted how alone I'd feel without them, but right now, my heart is a bleeding mess and I'm far more emotional than I'd like to be. At least the heat thing has dissipated. Being kidnapped and tortured seems to be the ideal cure for a cat in heat. I'm not surprised most cats prefer to live through the terrible hormonal tsunami that is heat rather than let themselves be catnapped.

I step out of the bedroom and right into a living room with a galley kitchen to my right. A long bench is hidden behind a table, a pillow and blanket thrown to one corner. Someone seems to have slept on the bench last night. I sniff the air. Benjamin.

A door at the other end of the room leads to a tiny bathroom and a second bedroom. That one smells of Lily and Bethany.

They're nowhere to be seen though. It's just me and the guys.

My stomach growls and I realise I've not eaten for far too long. I return to the kitchen and make a large pot of tea while rummaging through the cupboards. Most of the dishes are chipped, telling stories of many years of use.

I pick some random ingredients and throw them all in a pot. Right now, I don't really care whether you can combine potatoes, beets and dried up onions. Once the veggies are mostly cooked, I add the two eggs I found, plus whatever seasoning I can get my hands on. Most of the herb glasses don't have labels, so I hope I'm not poisoning us.

Ryker joins me and silently lays the table. He pours two glasses of water and one of milk. I hope that one's for me and not for him.

When I put the strange food mixture on the mismatched soup plates Ryker has prepared, Lennox comes out of the bedroom, wearing nothing but his boxers. His muscular chest smirks at me and reminds me that my heat isn't quite over yet.

I avert my eyes and start eating. Ryker pushes the glass of milk towards me. Good kitty. I empty it in one sip before continuing to shovel food into my mouth. Ryker looks similarly starved, while Lennox observes us with an amused grin.

"I'll get you some more milk," he says with a chuckle and tops up my glass. Good doggo.

We eat in silence, but there's no animosity between us. I understand why the two of them might doubt

Gryphon. They don't know him like I do. They've not fucked him... at least I hope they haven't. That would lead to all sorts of questions.

"This is surprisingly good," Ryker says in between bites. "Do I taste cardamom?"

I shrug. "I haven't got the faintest. If one of those little glasses contains cardamom, then yes, that's what you're tasting."

"She's never been much of a cook," Lennox stage-whispers. "Be glad she didn't give us raw potatoes."

I growl at him. "Once."

"Twice. Remember when you had to clean the kitchen and thought it would be fun to mess up the Pack meal plans?"

"Ah yes, I remember. That was fun."

I grin at the memory. I chopped up most of the potatoes that had been set aside for later in the week. Then I poured so much salt on them that they were inedible, but only until I realised I was hungry, so I pocketed some raw potato slices for Lennox and me to share.

We did a lot of things like that. Mostly me, especially after Lennox ran away. Of course, there were always consequences, but they were worth it.

"Is Little Kat safe?" I ask once I've finished my second plate of veggies.

Lennox nods. "I've checked on her every day. She doesn't know that you were held hostage; she thinks you're away on a secret mission. Better to stick with that mission."

"Understood. I'll go and visit her as soon as I've freed Gryphon."

The guys exchange a glance but don't say anything. Good. I'd hate to have to hurt them.

"Ryker, your cats are still watching him?"

He nods.

"Ask them where he is just now and have them lead me to him. I'd shift but I have a feeling that I'll need my strength."

"This is too dangerous," Lennox says slowly, as if he's afraid I might attack him if he says the wrong thing. "You need to rest and recover. Look at you, you're skin and bones and paler than a ghost. What you need is to stay here, eat lots and get some sunshine."

Ryker snickers. "You realise who you're talking to?"

The wolf shoots him a glare. "I know, but that doesn't make me give up hope. Deep inside, Kat might have an ounce of self-preservation left." He looks at me, his eyes filled with sadness. "Will you stay here if I ask you to? Will you promise me not to put yourself in danger?"

My heart screams at me to say yes, to give in to his puppy eyes, but no, I can't. "I'd do the same for you," I say, my voice choked at seeing him so emotional. "Both of you. I wouldn't abandon you and I can't abandon Gryphon either. He's one of mine and I protect what I own."

In any other situation, they'd probably protest to being called my property, but they wisely stay quiet.

Lennox keeps my eyes captured in his, then nods. "I'm coming with you."

"No, you can't. The Pack will want you too, same with Ryker. We can't give them all three of us."

Ryker gets up with a jolt, his chair tumbling to the ground. "And it's alright for you to give yourself to them?" He's shouting, his face a mask of anger. "And you want us to stand by and watch you sacrifice yourself?"

I reach out to him to calm him down, but he pushes my hand away.

"You can't go, Kat. I won't let you." He sighs and his voice quietens somewhat. "I can't lose you. You turned me into this, you showed me that I'm not alone. You unlocked my human side and right now, the human in me is begging you not to go."

I put a hand on his heaving chest and this time, he lets me. "And what does your cat say?"

He bows his head, regret reflecting in his glowing eyes. "That you need to protect your family, and that Gryphon is part of your clowder."

"Exactly. Don't worry, I'll be safe. I'll find Gryphon and I'll get him out of there. We'll come back and we'll live happily ever after. Okay?"

They both look at me and nod, but I have to fight back my tears because I'm making promises I'm not sure I can keep.

CHAPTER SEVENTEEN

I tuck at my collar, making sure the poison darts are safely secured. Bethany has supplied me with a new set, as well as with my knives. Her and Benjamin went back to the house where I'd been held to look around and found my weapons locked up in a chest. I run my hands over their hilts. It's good to have them back. I feel empty without them, even though I know I could shift and have claws much more effective than knives.

I'm following Pan, a beautiful ginger female, one of Ryker's closest friends. She leads the way, bringing me to where Gryphon was last spotted. The cats have been keeping an eye on him round the clock, whenever he left the building. It's handy to have them on board, although it's strange that Gryphon hasn't tried to make contact with them. He knows they spy for me, so it would be easy for him to pass them a message. He's stayed quiet though, probably afraid that he might be caught. If they let him walk free, that means he's convinced them he's on their side. He'll have to keep playing his role until they believe him fully. Why is he doing it though? Is he planning to stay with them for a while to find out their biggest weaknesses? Or is he hoping to attack from within?

I can't wait to talk to him. Not having him near me is like a physical ache. Must be my feline hormones doing that to me.

Pan brings me close to the Pack headquarters, where another cat is waiting for us behind some large bins. It's James, his extremely straight tail nervously bumping from left to right. He's a small but feral looking Bengal with round brown spots on his back and delicate stripes around his neck. A true beauty.

James meows, conveying his greetings. Pan rubs against him, then runs off without saying goodbye. Cats. Not the politest beings.

The Bengal leads me through a narrow alleyway full of rubbish and broken furniture until we get to a high wall that doesn't seem to belong to any of the buildings around us. Of course, I've been here before, but this wall is new. When I left the Pack over half a year ago, this wall didn't exist yet. Back then, I was able to walk along the alley to a hidden gate that leads into the sleeping quarters of some of the Pack members. Now, the way is blocked.

James gives me an encouraging meow.

"Want me to climb over there?" I ask and he nods, rolling his eyes at my perceived stupidity. Before I can ask any more questions, he runs off, leaving me alone. Alrighty then. This is the moment my men have warned me about. I could still turn back. There might be other ways to get Gryphon out of there. I could even wait for nightfall to hide in the shadows.

But no. I need him now. I'm not patient enough to wait. Call it me being reckless. Or an idiot.

I take a deep breath, check my weapons one last time - including all of the ones hidden beneath my clothes - and climb up the wall. My senses tell me that nobody is waiting on the other side, so that's a good sign. Although of course it would have been nice if Gryphon had come here, ready to be brought home. Why is life never that easy?

Beyond the wall, the alley continues, the same as on the other side, just without all the rubbish. Careful not to make any noise, I let myself drop to the ground and continue on, keeping close to the wall to my right, sinking into the shadows. It's mid-afternoon, but the sun is already beginning to drench the world in shades of orange and red. A beautiful light. I bet it's going to be a gorgeous sunset. Hopefully, I'll still be alive to admire it.

I grimace at my pessimistic thoughts and push them out of my mind. I need to focus. Switch on my assassin mindset, the one where my heart stops feeling and my brain does all the thinking. Cold, detached, merciless. That's who I need to be today.

To save others, you sometimes have to turn off your humanity. Or to make money, but that doesn't sound as nice.

The gate that used to lead into the Pack headquarters is now sealed shut and blocked with stones from the other side. I'm a bit confused about why the cats led me here. I don't know of any other way in from this alley. There are many different routes I could have taken, but James specifically brought me here.

There's nothing at the end of the alley, just the back wall of a house without any doors or windows. Am I involved in some kind of practical joke? Did Ryker tell the cats to lead me astray to distract me from something?

When I get my fingers on that overgrown kitty...

A strange scratching noise to my right makes me swirl around, my daggers at the ready. It comes from an unremarkable brick wall, part of one of the shabby houses in this area. I stay frozen, watching and observing. The scratching continues, then, suddenly, one of the bricks moves. It wobbles a little, then turns, exposing a hole in the wall. More bricks start to move aside, until the hole is big enough to let a cat in or out. Curious. I never knew this was here, and I lived in this place all my life. Well, until my life actually started for good.

I wait for someone to appear on the other side of the opening, or to say something, but nothing happens. Sniffing the air brings me a myriad of smells, none of them easy to identify. A lot of people have passed through here, both shifters and humans, but there isn't anyone waiting for me. How strange. It must be some kind of mechanism that started making this hole.

It's not quite big enough yet to let me climb into the house, so I randomly start touching the bricks and feel for the hidden technology that has caused them to move. When I reach the very first brick that moved, it starts shaking and the process continues. Must have got stuck.

More and more stones shift until the hole is just large enough for a small human. My men wouldn't be able to squeeze through, but luckily, I'm not as big as them. As a panther, I'd get stuck, but as a human, I just about manage to get through without too many scrapes. As soon as I'm inside the dark room, the mechanism begins again, faster this time, until the wall is back to how it used to be. Nobody would ever suspect it to be anything but a dull brick wall. I'm amazed. I want one of those.

Yet another windowless room awaits me, but this time, there's a door. The rest of the floor is covered in a thick layer of dust, but the passage between the trapdoor and the door is well used. I wonder if this way into the Pack headquarters has always been there or if they only installed it after that wall was built. No matter, I found it and now I'm on the way in.

The next room is full of discarded clothes. The floor is literally covered in them. This must be a sort of changing room. Ever heard of a wardrobe? And here was me thinking that I was untidy. This is a whole new level.

With all of the clothes giving off a myriad of scents, I have trouble focusing on what my senses are telling me. Has Gryphon been here? I can't tell. He might have, but it's just as likely that he hasn't. I know his scent well, but this is like trying to find a cat hair in a bag of hay.

This time, there's a window. I sneak towards it, keeping my head low. The glass is stained and the corners are home to several spiders and their respective cobwebs. Despite that, I recognise where I am. That courtyard down below is where we did our first training sessions. They were mostly beatings, our trainers showing us where it hurt the most so that we would be experts by the time we had to inflict pain on others. That was their excuse, anyway. I think they just liked beating us.

This part of the compound is for the youngest Pack members or those who've only recently arrived. I remember this area being heavily guarded, but strangely enough, I can't see a single person outside, and with all the sweaty clothes surrounding me, I can't use my sense of smell to detect threats. I'm relying on my eyes and sight alone. I don't like it. A cat's nose is one of her most important weapons and right now, I'm nose-blind.

I stay here for a few minutes, crouched beneath the window frame, watching for signs of life outside. Nobody to be seen. Have they abandoned this part of the headquarters? Did they maybe become scared after I burned down their research facility and killed everyone in those two houses last night?

I'm kind of disappointed. I came here to kill. Instead, I'm covered in dust and yucky smells.

When I'm sure nobody is hiding outside, I climb down the ladder at the other end of the room - a bit nicer than the rope earlier - and sneak through the room below. This one actually has a door, hurray!

Again, there are discarded clothes, supplies and even some weapons. When I was part of the Pack, they always made us keep our things in tiptop condition and meticulously sorted in our lockers. Leaving our clothes strewn on the floor like this would have earned us at least two weeks in solitary confinement, or worse. What is going on? I would have heard about a leadership change in the Pack. I might keep away from them, but most of the criminal underworld doesn't. I'd have been told by my contacts.

The door is the only way out of this building, unless I went upstairs again and climbed out of the window. As much as I love running around roofs, I know this compound well enough to decide to stay on the ground. There are watchful eyes everywhere and it's easier to hide inside the buildings rather than on top of them.

I mentally ready myself for a fight, then throw open the door and run to the building opposite the courtyard. Nobody rushes me. No alarming scents. Nothing. It's as if everyone's simply run away and left this place empty.

I make my way deeper into Pack territory. I know my way around and take the most hidden shortcuts I can remember, staying in the shadows as much as I can. The absence of people is beginning to make my skin itch. I hate not knowing what's going on.

By the time I get to my old dormitory, even the sound of my own footsteps makes me jump. This is beginning to feel like a big mistake.

At least this room makes it obvious that there are still people living here. Children's belongings are on the beds, mostly toys they've made themselves from rags and sticks. Lennox made me a doll once, which I promptly assassinated. To be fair, I didn't know any better. And to stay honest, I'd do the same thing again today. By now he should have figured out that I'm not a doll sort of girl. Unless the doll bleeds, screams and can pretend to die.

The kitchen not far from the dormitory smells of food and there's still something cooking in one of the pots. As if they all left within a moment's notice. Was I that reason?

It's not like I didn't know they'd likely set a trap for me, but this feels a little excessive.

The smells in the air make me hungry again, reminding me how I've not had enough to eat in the past few days. I've got some making up to do, but not now. Once Gryphon is safe, we can all do that date and have lots to eat in a fancy restaurant. I never asked the guys if they managed to save some money when the house exploded. There's some in the bank as well, under a fake name, but we had a lot of cash stashed away in my office. I don't care much for money and material things, but to build a new life and find ourselves a new home, we'll need it.

Suddenly, a scream echoes through the building. I raise my daggers, ready to jump, before realising the sound came through the speakers installed in every room in the compound. Another scream, and sadly, I know exactly whose scream it is.

Gryphon.

There's only one reason why they'd broadcast his pain over the loudspeakers and that's me. Fuck. It's just like I thought. They've made everyone leave so that I'd wander all the way into the centre of their headquarters, then they'll cut off my escape route and surround me from all sides. It's pretty much how I would have done it, but my fear for Gryphon has made me cocky. That's why assassins should never get attached. Love makes you stupid and predictable.

Not that I love him.

Obviously not.

"Where are you?" I shout, no longer trying to keep to the shadows. "Where is Gryphon?"

The screams stop abruptly, followed by a very familiar voice.

"Step outside into the assembly yard."

It's Elder Grimsay, one of the most feared Pack members. I've only ever seen him twice face to face, but everyone here knows his voice. He likes to do speeches, especially before and after public punishments. I heard him talk most days while growing up about how all shifters are abominations and need to be trained by the Pack. At the very beginning, I believed him. That's what they do. Destroy your self-confidence, make you convinced that you're something inferior and that the only way to deal with my feral, non-human side is to be controlled by the Pack.

Of course, I stopped believing that pretty quickly, once I saw what they did to us. Other shifters weren't as lucky. They kept on listening to Grimsay's words, convinced that they were the disgusting monsters he was calling us. Those are the dangerous, deluded and often stupid members of the Pack. And I'm very likely surrounded by them.

This was such a bad idea, but it's too late to turn back. I'm either going to get out of here with Gryphon in tow, or I'm going to be taken by the people I both hate and fear most in the world. I prefer the former option.

I know my knives won't do much good against the assembled might of the Pack, but I grip them tight nonetheless, readying myself for a fight. Taking one last deep breath, I step outside, into the assembly yard.

Among the scents of shifters and humans, one stands out. Gryphon. He's close. I keep my back close to a wall, making sure nobody can sneak up on me from behind.

And then he's there. Gryphon. He walks out of a building opposite, wearing a tight suit and not looking at all as if he's just been tortured. He smiles at me, but the usual warmth in his eyes is missing.

He slowly strides towards me, his gaze fixed on me as if he's trying to hold me in place with his eyes alone. The way he moves… a predator about to pounce on his prey. My back prickles and I know people are watching us from all directions. They want to know what he does next, just as I do.

My stomach churns at the coldness he's looking at me with. This isn't my Gryphon, the man who made me laugh, who made his music caress me, who fought by my side. This isn't even his siren. This is something new.

Please let it be an act. Please let it be a mask that he's going to drop any second now before escaping together.

"Kat," he says in a strangely emotionless voice. "Thanks for coming."

"Of course I was going to come. Let's turn and run before they can catch us."

He smirks, and the look he gives me turns even darker.

"I'm not going to run with you. This is my home."

Just like that, he breaks my heart. I can almost hear it shattering.

I stare at him, still clutching onto the vain hope that this is an act, a joke.

He's close enough now that I can reach out to touch him, but I don't. It doesn't feel right. As much as I want to hug him, this isn't my Gryphon.

For a moment, something flickers in his bright green eyes, the opposite of the ice he's shown me so far. He closes the distance between us, and I expect anything to happen, anything but him putting a collar around my neck.

CHAPTER EIGHTEEN

I expect to be in instant pain, but all I feel is a strange cold seeping into my bones. My mind turns foggy, but I can still concentrate on my surroundings.

"The collar Doctor Fitzroy put on you in the lab was a prototype," Gryphon explains as if he can read my mind. "One that could be remote controlled. This one is an older model, but it's more reliable and a lot less painful."

I glare at him. "Do you want me to be grateful that you put this on me?"

He shrugs. "It would be a start. The more you cooperate, the less it will hurt."

I step over the shards of my broken heart and slap him, hard. Surprised, he holds his cheek, then starts laughing.

"I guess I deserved that."

This must be a clone. This can't be my Gryphon. Did they replace his brain? Or is he on some kind of drugs? My Gryphon wouldn't let me hit him. He'd also not grin at me with that arrogant, cold glint in his eyes.

I rub the collar, still surprised at how it's not taking away my ability to think. A dumb pain is starting to build at the back of my head, but it's not distracting me as of yet.

"Come with me," Gryphon commands. I snarl at him, but all he does is smirk. What a bastard. I realise I still have my knives in my hands and I could easily stab him, but this is still Gryphon. Somewhere is the Gryphon who rocked inside me, who held me in his arms, who listened to me talking about random and probably disturbing stuff. I can't kill him. As much as my assassin mind wants to, my heart is refusing to even consider the possibility. Even if that means that I'll be their prisoner. Or worse. I won't harm Gryphon.

He seems to realise the moment I make that decision and something flares in his eyes. Triumph. I drop my arms and push my knives into their sheaths. I'm amazed he's not disarmed me yet. That would have been the first thing I would have done in his position.

"Follow me."

It's an order, but he's not reinforcing his command. Besides putting the collar on me, he's not laid his hands on me. Maybe he's been told not to, or maybe there's a tiny spark of goodness left in him.

"Where to?"

"The elders want to see you."

He starts walking and I follow him, even though I know the route and could easily lead the way. I've only ever been in the Elders' Hall once, when I graduated from being an apprentice to a trained assassin. Only the leaders of the Pack and their closest associates are allowed in there.

I take one last wistful look at the red-tinged sky, then step into the building, leaving my freedom behind.

We walk past guards who are staring at me as if I'm the worst threat they've ever faced. I recognise a few, but none of them signals that they know me. Not that I was ever friends with anyone in the Pack after Lennox left. I had my heart broken once and made sure that was never going to happen again. Despite that, I force myself to smile at the guards I know from when I still lived here, giving them short nods. One, Gerrard, has the decency to look away, but the others just ignore my gesture and continue to stare at me as if I'm about to go on a killing spree. Which isn't all that far from the truth. If Gryphon wasn't here, behaving strangely, and if I weren't wearing a collar, I'd make short process of them all. I'm not sure if I should kill them all, or leave some alive, the ones who I know are reluctant Pack members rather than fervent followers.

While the guards at the entrance and in the corridors are collared, the two standing in front of the large doors leading into the Elder's Hall aren't forced to wear them. They're here voluntarily, they've been brainwashed enough that nobody is expecting them to ever switch sides. I don't understand them. Why would you ever choose to be a captive? I'd rather be poor, persecuted and hunted than live in a prison of my own choosing.

Gryphon doesn't look back, confident that I'm

following him. It's not as if I have a choice, unless I want to die prematurely. The way the guards look at me and grip their weapons doesn't leave any doubt to their orders. If I run, I'm dead.

No thanks.

One of the uncollared guards knocks on the doors, then stands back and pulls back his shoulders. His head may be straight, but his eyes are following my every movement. I don't think I've ever seen him before. Just goes to show how much has changed since I left, and how much I didn't know about the Pack while I was still living here.

"Try not to insult them," Gryphon says under this breath as the doors open. That kind of makes me want to do the exact opposite, but I bite my tongue and follow him inside, towards the large table where the Elders are waiting for us.

There are nine of them, but only seven are present. Grimsay is sitting in the centre, staring at me from under bushy brows. To his left are two women, both of them unknown to me, and a young man that seems familiar but I can't remember his name. To Grimsay's right is George Kenny, the Elder that was responsible for assassin assignments and who I therefore know quite well, and the Terrifying Twins. They're brother and sister, looking innocent as fuck with their elegant clothes and polished expressions. They deserve their name, though. Since they're responsible for discipline and punishments, I've spent my fair time with them. I'd hoped to never see them again. They still occasionally appear in my nightmares, but seeing them in the flesh makes a shiver of fear run down my back. I thought I'd moved past my fear of them. There are few things in life that I'm afraid of, but those two are top of my list.

"I brought her here as requested," Gryphon says smoothly and bows before the Elders. Disgusting. If they expect me to bow, they're going to have to break my knees first. From the look Grimsay is giving me as I stare him down, he's considering it.

Elder Kenny gives Gryphon a smile. "Well done. If we had any doubts about your loyalty, you've now proven what side you're on. I'll be writing to your father."

Gryphon inclines his head. "I appreciate it. All I've ever wanted is to make him proud."

Am I allowed to puke? This is cringeworthy. My Gryphon would never behave like this.

If they know his father, at least part of what he said is true. They're sirens, either all or some of them. It's hard to tell, but now that I know what to look for, they do look a little too flawless to be human, especially the people to Grimsay's left.

Grimsay is still returning my glare and the hatred in his eyes is almost too much to bear looking at. "You've caused us a lot of trouble. Far more than your creators ever expected. And trust me, if Boris and Professor Lakefield hadn't assured me that it was all under control and important for the experiment's results, I would have put an end to you a long time ago."

Boris, that was the blond man who I killed in the blue house. Good riddance.

"When the professor died, I was close to terminating

you," Elder Grimsay continues," but once again, the scientists told me it was vital that we kept you alive. That was until you started learning the truth and destroyed one of our labs. I'm afraid this is the end of the line, K1."

I'm going to kill him just for that. I have a name. I'm not a number.

Even though the collar mutes my senses, I have no trouble noticing that Gryphon's heartbeat is speeding up. Does that mean he actually cares about what's happening to me? Or is he simply excited to witness my execution?

The man to the very left smiles at me, but there's no warmth in his expression. I finally recognise him; he was on one of the photos I was shown while I was chained down to that chair. His dark brown hair is combed back with precision, his thick glasses pushed all the way up his nose. In the photograph, he was wearing a lab coat, so he must be one of the scientists. It's surprising that he's one of the Elders, considering his age. Maybe he's a bit of a genius.

"It's a pity I'll never get the chance to perform all the tests I'd planned." There is genuine regret in his voice, but I doubt it's because I'm about to be killed. It's because I won't be available for his experiments. "Professor Lakefield didn't approve of all of them, but now that he's been disposed of, I was hoping I'd finally get the opportunity."

"Wait, disposed of?" I ask before I can stop myself.

A wry smile curves Grimsay's lips. "Our head scientist was getting attached to his subjects. He was becoming a liability. We no longer knew if his experiments were actually beneficial to our aims or if he was simply doing them to satisfy his own curiosity and strange sense of morality."

They killed one of their own. Not that I'm surprised, but from what I'd heard of Professor Lakefield, I would have assumed that he was too important to get rid of. After all, he was the one who'd started the whole cloning project together with Doctor Fitzroy.

At least now I know that Mystery Man aka Lakefield really is dead. Who knows, maybe he even left me the house without the Pack being aware of that. If his daughter really exists. She might be a fake, employed by the Pack to deceive me.

Grimsay looks around the table. "Who wants to do it?"

The twins grin and reply at the same time. "Me."

I repress a growl. Their scent smells of cruelty. They won't make it quick or painless. They're going to make me suffer and draw out my death as much as they possibly can.

Bring it on. I'm not going to let them kill me without a fight.

Elder Grimsay looks at the twins for a moment, his brow furrowed as if he's wondering whether that's a good idea. Then he nods and turns to Gryphon.

"You can step away from here now, although you should really have removed her weapons. Is the collar secure? We don't want a repeat of yesterday's events."

He's calling me murdering a dozen people an 'event'. Only shows how dangerous he is, how much lives are worth to the Pack. I killed their people and yet he doesn't seem very concerned.

Gryphon steps behind me and puts his hands on my collar. I freeze, hating him touching me. Traitor. I'm tempted to pull one of my knives and gut him. But even knowing that my death is imminent, my weak, idiotic heart betrays me, fixing me in place. I can't kill him.

I realise the change before I hear the click of the collar opening. Power streams into my body and my mind clears, becoming as sharp as ever.

The collar falls to the stone floor, echoing into the stunned silence.

"Shift," Gryphon whispers, before pulling my knives from their sheaths and running towards the Elders.

CHAPTER NINETEEN

My surprise is enough to make me hesitate for a moment, but when I see Gryphon plunge one of my knives into the young scientist's heart, my training takes over. I shift in one fluid motion, jumping forward before I'm even fully shifted. My claws extend, sharp and deadly.

All I can think about is that there is a lot of prey in this room that needs killing.

The Elders are on their feet, surrounding Gryphon, but just like he's always said, most sirens aren't trained to fight. One of the women haphazardly swings a sword around, looking like she has no clue what she's doing. Gryphon cuts her throat with a simple swipe of his dagger, quicker than she can raise her blade. Two down, five more to go, and that's before I've even joined the fray.

I focus on the twins, who I know are good at fighting. They used to spar in the training yard and while they're not the best assassins, they do pose a challenge. I roar and they turn to me, ignoring Gryphon. That still leaves him with three others, but neither Elder Grimsby nor the woman is very competent with their weapons. George Kenny makes up for their lack of skills, though. He's trained generations of assassins and has a lot of tricks up his sleeve. I need to deal with the twins soon so that I can join Gryphon.

The woman manages to mostly block my attack with her shield (she's the only one I know who fights with a sword and shield like a knight), but my impact is enough to make her stumble backwards and I swipe her legs with one paw before the can regain her balance. Her brother swings his cutlass at me, but I evade him easily, predicting his move as soon as he starts it. I've watched them fight for years, and they seem to have forgotten that. I know how they like to fight when they're two against one. If one of them is on the defensive, the other will distract their opponent, keeping them busy until both twins can attack at once.

Instead of involving him in a fight, I keep attacking his sister, standing on my hind legs for a moment only to let myself drop down, pushing against her chest with my paws, making her fall to the ground. Expecting the brother's attack, I roll to my left, and, just as I'd hoped, his cutlass slices into the woman's leg where I'd been a second ago. Bingo.

She screams, shouting at her brother in pain and disbelief. He freezes, shocked, giving me the perfect opportunity to rush him, toppling him and clamping my jaws around his neck. His sister screams when I rip out his throat, shaking his body like a rag doll. She tries to get up, but her injured leg makes her sluggish and I'm upon her before she can defend herself.

I'd love to make this slow and painful, but I'm very aware that Gryphon is still fighting. I listen for heartbeats. He still has two opponents.

The doors bang open, reminding me that there will be guards running at us any second now. Guards who will be better trained than the Elders. We need to hurry.

With a loud growl, I run my sharp teeth along the woman's jugular, making sure she can see my eyes while I kill her. After all the pain she's inflicted on me, I want me to be the last thing she sees.

I turn and race towards Gryphon before the final flicker of life has fully extinguished. There's no time to savour her death. Maybe I'll dream of her tonight, a different version of her demise where I had an hour or two to slowly make her pay for all she's done to me. This was too fast and not at all satisfying.

Gryphon is on the defensive, both Elder Kenny and Grimsay fighting him at once. Grimsay isn't the best swordsman, but he's good enough to distract Gryphon from the opponent that actually matters.

I roar as loud as I can, making both of them turn instinctively. That's enough for Gryphon to get the upper hand, launching a flurry of strikes against Kenny. Grimsay turns to me and I show my teeth in delight. It's going to be fun killing him. He deserves it in so many ways.

As much as I want to play with my food, the guards have almost reached us. Bowmen are taking up position by the door, but for now, we're moving too fast for them to risk shooting. They'd be boiled alive for hurting an Elder. If they're lucky.

I draw on my new strength, that secret well that I've only just discovered, and move faster than it should be physically possible. I bite his sword arm, making his weapon fall to the ground, while at the same time using one paw to slice open his abdomen. The squelching sound of his entrails sliding out makes me smile, before ripping off some of his fingers.

He howls in pain, dropping to his knees, trying to keep his innards from spreading all over the floor. I think he's not quite noticed his missing digits yet. Either way, he's done for. I leave him to it, safe in the knowledge that he's going to die soon and that he's in no condition to fight me.

Gryphon is duelling George Kenny, their blades meeting in quick succession. It's beautiful to behold and to be honest, I think it would be unfair to deprive Gryphon of it, so instead of butting in, I take on the guards. With a mighty roar, I start running, ploughing into them claws first, ripping and cutting and biting. It's carnage. Some of them manage to give me small cuts, but I'm too fast for them to strike me properly. I kill them faster than they can enter the room. It doesn't take long until I'm surrounded by corpses. Their blood coats my fur, my tongue, even my whiskers. I'm going to need a wash later on, but for now, I'm savouring that beautiful taste. Almost makes me want to nibble a little. It's like I'm standing in the middle of an all-you-can-eat buffet and it keeps getting refilled, all I need to do is cut their throats a little.

Meat always tasted best when it's had the chance to bleed dry for a bit.

"Kat!"

Gryphon's voice slowly pulls me from my frenzy. I blink a couple of times, taking in the scene. Elder Kenny is on the ground, severely injured, his heart still beating but about to stop forever. Gryphon seems fine, apart from a few shallow wounds, just like the ones I have. I can already feel mine healing; that always itches. How annoying.

More guards are approaching the room from afar, but for now, we've killed everyone inside. For one siren and one cat, we've done pretty well.

"What do we do now?" Gryphon asks as I slowly stalk towards him. "I never thought further than this. I had a hard time believing I'd ever even manage to get to this point, so it seemed irrelevant to make plans. Do we torch this place? Kill as many people as we can? Take off everyone's collars? Leave and let them sort out themselves?"

I love how he gets a tiny little dimple when he's deep in thought. But no, I can't think of how cute he is. He betrayed me, he deceived me, even though it turns out he didn't. Not really. It's kind of hard to tell.

Since I can't talk, I flash my teeth at him and give him an angry glare. To underline my point, I throw an arm at him - not mine, just a random one lying in a pool of blood on the floor. Some limbs lost their owners during the battle. Or maybe it's the other way round. Either or, nobody cares. Those people all fought on the wrong side and died because of it.

Yes, many of them are wearing collars, but they could have resisted. Not everyone can withstand a collar's command for longer than a minute or so, but that minute would have been enough for me to spare them. Not a single one of them did that, though. I would have smelled their agitation. No, all of them fought for the Pack and against me.

As much as I would like to raze the entire compound to the ground, I know there are people here who aren't blind followers. They're likely amongst the guards about to spill into the room. They have managed to resist the command for a while, but couldn't do it any longer. And then there are the children and teenagers. I couldn't kill any of them, no matter how brainwashed they are. But what to do with them? It's not like we can just remove their collars. They'd go feral and it would likely end in a blood bath. Lennox said that when his collar was taken off for the first time, he'd been out of his mind for a long time. I only held on to my rational mind because Mystery Man was there to guide me.

I shudder at the memory. Of course, he knew how the collars worked. He'd been working with the woman who developed them. I was such a fool to trust him.

"What are we doing?" Gryphon asks, pulling me back to the task at hand. Not that I can answer him. "And yes, I'm sorry, but let's talk about that once we're out of here."

I growl at him again and he lifts his hands as if he wants to defend himself. "I meant none of what I said, alright? I never planned to hurt you, I never betrayed you, and I only did it so that we could get close to the

Elders and get rid of them. You'll get the full apology later, I promise. But now we need to act. I bet all the important people that weren't in this room are either fleeing or on the way to eliminate us. As much as I enjoyed this, I don't fancy facing off with every capable Pack assassin. We'd not survive that."

As much as it hurts, I agree with him. So far, the actual assassins have kept back and let the guards do the fighting. Having been one of them, I'm aware most of them are shifters who were forced to become what they are now. I don't want to kill them, and yet, we're in no position to deal with them all right now. If there were lots of us, dozens and dozens, we could work on first killing all the bad people, and then taking off collars one by one, while staying with the shifters to make sure they don't go feral. That would be the ideal plan. Sadly, there's only Gryphon and me. I think the clean-up has to wait for another day.

It's time to retreat and regroup. We've done the most critical part, cutting the head off the snake, and dealing with its twitching body doesn't seem as important now.

I meow, then realise he won't understand, so I simply turn towards the exit and start walking through the lake of blood, ignoring the eyes of the dead staring up at me.

Our family awaits us in front of our new home. Bethany, Benjamin, Lily, Lennox and Ryker. How far I've come from being all on my own.

The wagon looks small from the outside, especially with all of them standing outside, looking at us expectantly, but at least our bed should be just about big enough for four. I can always sleep on top of one of them.

They want answers, of course, and I let Gryphon deal with that while I shift back to human. He gives them the quick version – how he was first held against his will with me as the incentive to make him behave, but how he managed to get them to trust him once they found out who his family is. How he carefully led them to come up with a plan that involved him as the bait. How he figured out how to only partially close a collar.

I only listen with one ear, too busy picking bone splinters from between my teeth.

Ryker snickers when I start trying to get rid of the blood under my fingernails. "Kat, you need a wash."

While my Meow employees make some food, I disappear in the shower with Lennox and Ryker. They seem very interested in making sure I don't have blood in my hair, on my breasts, between my legs... they check my entire body from top to bottom, again and again. Their fingers dance on my skin, bringing me to new heights that crescendo into a concert of groans as I make sure that they know much I love their attention.

When we return to the kitchen, hair wet and only wrapped in a towel each, Lily is talking to someone at the door. Please don't let it be related to our little Pack massacre. I need a break and a lot of food.

Lily waves to me, her face surprisingly pale. "Kat, you've got visitors."

I shoot her a confused look – I'm not used to seeing Lily this flustered – and join her by the door.

And look at myself.

Twice.

"She really looks like us," one of the girls says to the other.

"She does. Like she's our twin."

"She's too old to be our twin."

"An older sister then."

The other girl nods and they both turn to me, grinning with exactly the same smile I see every day in the mirror.

"Hey, big sister."

~ **The End** ~

But no, not really! This was planned as a trilogy, but of course, it never turns out as planned… Kat's story continues in Hisss.

Keep up to date with all my releases by subscribing to my newsletter: skyemackinnon.com/newsletter.

And if you're looking for your next post-Kat read, take a look at my Kilts & Kisses box set, combining the first books in three of my series (basically, you're getting three books for the price of one, hurray): books2read.com/kiltsandkisses

Meow, amazing reader!

I hope you enjoyed reading Purrr as much as I did writing it. Kat is probably my favourite heroine just now and I kind of wish I could be like her. Sans the heat problem. That kind of wasn't planned and it surprised me a little, but then, nothing in this series is ever planned. Kat just won't let me stick to the ideas I have for her. She wanted to be in heat (kind of), so it happened. I'd not really intended to have that much steaminess in this book, but again, she demanded it. If you prefer less steamy urban fantasy, please forgive me. If you came here for the sex, I hope you enjoyed it.

This series was planned as a trilogy, but of course Kat decided that she needed more. She's selfish like that. That also means that I got to write another cliffhanger (yay!) and have my designer make an amazing fourth cover. Wait until you see it, it's gorgeous.

Covers are one of my favourite things about books. Some covers I buy from designers, some I make myself and others are made by my dear friend and co-author Arizona Tape (she does covers as Vampari Designs). A cover is how this series started in the first place. I saw this beautiful cover featuring a redhead and a panther. As a fan of both cats and red hair (sadly my sister got those genes and I'm stuck with boring brown), I just had to get it, even though I didn't have a story back then. First, I thought the panther might be the woman's sidekick, but when I thought about it, I realised I really wanted a heroine with the characteristics of a cat. And that's how Meow was born.

Strange to think that a single image kickstarted this series… plus my love of cats. I used to have two cats, Muffin and her daughter Lily (also known as Crumbs since she never really grew to full size), who were both as feline as you can imagine. Arrogant queens who expected to be spoiled, waited on and left alone when they couldn't be bothered with humans.

As you'll realise, Lily made it into this book as a human (well, succubus). Muffin too, but her name didn't seem to fit, so I sneaked her in as someone else… I wonder whether I should tell you who it is. Should I? Mmhm… I'll say his much: she's neither human nor a cat.

By the way, I've loved receiving all your messages, cat memes and reviews for Catnip Assassins, keep them coming, they're my own personal catnip. Every time you leave a review or recommend the book to a friend, Kat purrrrrs. Probably. She might be busy with her men, now that they're reunited.

Anyway, I just wanted to say thanks for sticking with

this series. By reading my books, you not only help me write full time (to give you even more books), but you also feed my bunnies (who're almost like cats) and refill my dried mango supply. I need that to write, in combination with far too much tea (with milk, obviously, I'm not a psychopath).

If you need more books to add to your list, flick forward and take a look at my massive book list. No idea where they all came from. Books just seem to happen. And do stalk me on social media, I always love hearing from you.

Lots of love,

Skye

P.S. If you want to read chapters before they're published, get insider news and support my writing, take a look at my Patreon account: patreon.com/skyemackinnon.

ABOUT THE AUTHOR

Skye MacKinnon is a USA Today & International Bestselling Author whose books are filled with strong heroines who don't have to choose.

She embraces her Scottishness with fantastical Scottish settings and a dash of mythology, no matter if she's writing about Celtic gods, cat shifters, or the streets of Edinburgh.

When she's not typing away at her favourite cafe, Skye loves dried mango, as much exotic tea as she can squeeze into her cupboards, and being covered in pet hair by her two bunnies, Emma and Darwin.

Support her on Patreon and get exclusive benefits:
patreon.com/skyemackinnon

Subscribe to her newsletter:
skyemackinnon.com/newsletter

facebook.com/skyemackinnonauthor

twitter.com/skye_mackinnon

instagram.com/skyemackinnonauthor

bookbub.com/authors/skye-mackinnon

goodreads.com/SkyeMacKinnon

amazon.com/author/skye_mackinnon

www.ingramcontent.com/pod-product-compliance
Lightning Source LLC
Chambersburg PA
CBHW030622190726
48286CB00008B/2357